How to Flirt with a Hellhound

Hellhounds of Paradise Falls

Book 1

Shannon Mae

Formatting and cover design by Tammy, Aspen Tree E.A.S.
Editing by Shannon, Aspen Tree E.A.S.
Page edge design by Painted Wings Publishing Service

TABLE OF CONTENTS

ℭBLURB:

Toby

Maybe I have an overactive imagination, but the hot guy next door totally gives off serial killer vibes. Why else would he know how long it takes to bleed out from a wound? Yeah, ok, so I asked, but it was research. Being an author definitely makes for some odd questions (someone had better clear my browser history when I die, that's all I'm saying). It's not like I'm stalking my hot neighbor or anything—there's nothing wrong with watching him out my window. Although I might have my own stalker (and not the cute harmless kind), which is kind of terrifying. Even if he isn't a serial killer, maybe my seriously sexy neighbor whose eyes seem to glow red (a trick of the light, I'm sure) can help me out.

Dexter

How do you tell your cute neighbor that cutting off fingers probably won't cause a victim to bleed out? I don't know if trying out Toby's writing ideas is a good method of flirting, but there's just something about him that calls to my hellhound. He's adorable, awkward, and all kinds of clueless. He brings out my protective instincts, and I find myself wanting to please him, even if that means figuring out some of the answers to his rather bloodthirsty questions. When I find out Toby might actually be in danger, nothing will stop my hellhound from protecting him. He's mine, even if he doesn't know it, and I'll tear apart anyone who even thinks of hurting him.

Tags: Socially awkward writer and serial killer(ish) hellhound fall in love; talking about dismemberment totally counts as flirting, right?; there's death and maiming, but only of really bad people; Dex would literally burn the world down for those he cares about; Toby is adorably clueless; hellhounds have tails, and they know how to use them.

ACKNOWLEDGEMENTS

Thank you, as always, to my daughter. You are my biggest cheerleader, and I love you!

Thank you to Scott, who encouraged me to start this whole journey. I wouldn't be here without you!

Thank you to Jennifer Cody and Tammy B. from Aspen Tree EAS. You should both know by now how amazing you are! You both make each book better, and you both put up with my odd questions and ramblings. You guys are wonderful!!!

Thank you to Nicole, Molly O, and Elizabeth D for being the most awesome beta readers! Nicole—your feedback and corrections are always so appreciated, and I'm thankful you've been on this journey with me from the start! Molly O—I LOVE reading your messages! I know I've done a good job when the comments keep coming! Elizabeth—you are a grammar queen, and I thank you so much for finding all those typos that we somehow missed!

Thank you to Kirstin J (Liam) and Jessie J (Sebastien) from my Facebook group for name suggestions!

Finally, thank you to all my readers. Every message, every email, and every comment in my group keeps me going. Meeting some of you at signings was inspirational, and I am thankful for every one of you!

Reader Warning

This book is intended for mature audiences. It is a dark(ish) romance that discusses torture, death, and maiming (but only of very bad people). There are characters who have traumatic backstories, as well. These things occur, for the most part, off page, because I'm squeamish and can't watch horror movies without covering my eyes.

There are also some very steamy times between men. Those definitely take place on page, in full detail. All sex acts are completely consensual and fully enjoyed by everyone involved. And (as always) there's a tail, and the hellhound knows how to use it.

For a complete list of content warnings (including spoilers), please check the next page.

Content Warnings

- Discussions of various methods of torture, including maiming, dismemberment, flaying, bloodletting, and medieval torture devices (torture occurs off page)
- Violence
- House fire (minor villainous character)
- Implied abusive relationship (secondary character)
- Kidnapping (off page; secondary character)
- Human trafficking (off page; secondary character)
- Stalking
- Consensual biting, knotting, and tail play
- Mention of trauma, including homophobia, violence, and abuse (not graphic; Toby likes to make up vague but tragic backstories for people)

Chapter 1

"I think my neighbor is a serial killer," I whispered, peeking out from behind the drapes to the house next door.

"Toby, are you writing dark romances again?" Josh sighed.

"And," I added, ignoring his long-suffering tone, "I think his eyes glowed red the other night."

"So it's paranormal dark romances, then," he grumbled.

"I'm serious, Josh!" I defended, walking away from the window and heading into the kitchen to ruffle around in the pantry. There had to be… ah, there they were. Potato chips. Who needed a full meal when there were potato chips?

"You know, when I was in the yard the other day talking to my PA, I asked how long it took someone to bleed out from being stabbed in the stomach, and my neighbor was walking by, and he said, 'It depends on the depth of the wound and the size of the blade, so anywhere from a few short minutes to days.' And then he just kept on walking, like it was a totally normal conversation. Josh, who knows that sort of information and treats that as an everyday topic of conversation?" I asked, crunching on some chips.

"Are you eating potato chips? Toby, that isn't dinner," Josh groused.

"And do you remember when we had an hour long conversation on ways to be electrocuted?"

"Yeah, so?" I asked, ruffling through the bag for the chips that were curled. They totally tasted better when they were curled in half.

"So you, Toby. Someone like you knows that kind of information. He's probably a writer. Or maybe a doctor," Josh reassured me.

"Or a serial killer," I added, giving an "Aha!" as I found another curly chip.

Josh sighed again. "He's cute, isn't he?"

"OMG yes, he's totally hot. All big and strong and scary looking. He's tall, and I think he's got a couple tattoos, although sadly I haven't seen him with his shirt off. I can't wait for lawn mowing season," I admitted, still crunching away on my chips. "Not that I'll be mowing my lawn. Ohhh, do you think maybe I could get him to mow my lawn? That would be so hot."

"You want a serial killer mowing your lawn?" Josh asked.

"Hah!" I shouted into the phone. "You admit he's a serial killer!"

Josh sighed again. He had no appreciation for my mental prowess.

"Why don't they make bags of potato chips that are just curls? I bet people would buy them by the droves. The curly chips always taste better," I commented, shaking the bag around to look for more curly chips.

"They're called ruffles, Toby. Focus, please—we're talking about your non-serial killer neighbor," Josh reminded me.

"Nope. Ruffle chips are… Well, they're ruffled. Those aren't curls. These are like fully curled in half but they're straight chips," I said, crunching loudly.

Josh sighed again before asking, "Why do you think he's a serial killer? Aside from the tattoos, the hotness factor, and your current writing project?" Josh asked.

"I don't think he works. He's always coming and going at odd hours, and he wears a lot of black, because you know that hides the blood stains better…" I began.

"Or it's just his aesthetic," Josh cut in.

"And you know the house next door has a basement," I went on, totally ignoring him. "He blacked out the basement windows, but I see lights on down there at odd hours of the night. Plus, when I was up at like 2 am the other night, he was carrying a rolled up carpet or something into the house over his shoulder," I finished triumphantly.

"First of all, if his windows are blacked out, how can you tell the lights are on?" Josh asked.

"Duh, because a little light escapes," I said around a mouthful of chips.

"At this rate you won't have room for dinner," Josh warned me, but I ignored him, still crunching away. "And I'll give you that redecorating at 2 am is weird, but peeping on your neighbor at 2 am is also weird. One might even say stalkerish," Josh added.

"I am not a stalker!" I defended. "Being curious about one's neighbor is normal behavior!"

Josh laughed at that. "Toby, you know I love you, but you are definitely not normal."

I grunted around the chips in my mouth, rolling up the bag and going in search of a clip. I probably wouldn't have room for dinner, but I hated cooking for one person anyway, so I wasn't too worried about it.

"My point is that sometimes people do odd things. That doesn't mean they're serial killers. Or stalkers. I'm sure your neighbor is very nice, and if you had an actual conversation with him I'm sure you'd see that. And no, him commenting on stomach wounds does not qualify as a conversation," Josh said.

He was always so reasonable. Sometimes it was annoying.

"I ought to call Seb. He'll totally agree with me," I grumped.

"Yeah, maybe don't call him about your serial killer neighbor," Josh warned.

I immediately stopped what I was doing and leaned against the counter, focusing on the conversation. "Uh oh. What happened now?" I asked.

"Apparently he was out on a date and the guy at the next table had a heart attack and died," Josh sighed.

"Aww, man. He hasn't been on a date in ages. I'm guessing it didn't go well after that?" I asked. Poor Seb. He did not have good luck.

"Nope. He performed CPR until the paramedics got there, even though he said the guy was gone. And you know Seb—nothing fazes him. I think there could be a zombie apocalypse and he'd be asking if we felt like going out for ice cream in that cheery tone of his," Josh said.

I snorted. It was true. Seb was probably the happiest person I knew, despite the fact that people were always dying around him. And yes, he worked in a hospital, so it was kind of expected that he'd see some death, but people seemed to die around him outside of work all the time too. It was amazing the guy didn't get a complex.

"So he went back to his table and started eating dinner again," Josh went on, "and his date was all shocked and asked him how he could eat after that. I think the guy said something about him being heartless, which is crazy. Seb is the sweetest guy I know. Anyway, I told Seb obviously a guy who was that blind didn't deserve him, but Seb was pretty bummed."

"Yeah." It was my turn to sigh. "I wish we could find someone for him. I know he's lonely."

It was a shame that Seb and I wouldn't work out, but we just weren't each other's type. We were far too similar, and the only chemistry between us was the course we'd taken together in college. Where someone had died, by the way. Lab accident, although their death hadn't been immediate. I'd looked it up later, and I hadn't told Seb. I didn't want my friend to actually get a complex.

"Maybe your serial killer neighbor?" Josh joked. "I mean, people dropping dead around Seb wouldn't scare him off if he really is a serial killer."

"Nope. I get first dibs on serial killer hottie," I announced.

Josh laughed, and we said our goodbyes. Josh was supposed to go meet his boyfriend, who I didn't much like, for dinner. The guy just gave me creep vibes, but I knew Josh wouldn't listen. I might have an overactive imagination, but that didn't mean I was totally wrong about people.

With that I walked out of the kitchen and back into the living room to look out the side window at my serial killer's house. There was no fence until the backyards, and I had a pretty clear view of next door. His car was there, so I knew he was home. I pushed the curtain aside, and then I nearly screamed when I saw my neighbor staring out his window at my house.

"Shit!" I yelped, dropping onto the floor and out of sight.

And oh my god, if that wasn't the stupidest reaction ever. I peeked up over the window, and yup, he was still there, staring at my window with a slight smirk on his face. I sat up a bit more and gave a wave, pointing down and trying to make some vague motion that I had fall-en.

Not sure he bought it. He just looked amused, and I gave a random shrug and waved again before sliding over to the side of the window and bumping my head against the wall a few times.

"Nice job, Toby. Now the hot serial killer neighbor will totally think you're a stalker," I mumbled to myself.

Chapter 2

Dexter

I couldn't help the slight smile on my face as thumps were followed by Toby's comment. If the poor man knew how good my hearing was, he would probably die of mortification. He was quite dramatic like that, but I found myself amused by it.

Which was rather odd for me.

It isn't that I didn't enjoy life, because I did. My enjoyment was just… flavored a bit differently than most.

I waited until I heard Toby get up and his footsteps took him upstairs. I watched the light turn on in the window I knew led to his bedroom, and when the light finally went off, I moved.

Stalkerish? Probably. But I felt oddly protective of my next door neighbor. My brain was equating him with pack at this point, and I didn't fight my instincts. Toby was mine to protect, whether he knew it or not.

With that thought, I made my way to the basement, leaving the light off tonight. I could see just as well without it, and the main area where I worked was a soundproof booth that had separate lighting.

I opened it up to see the naked man hanging from the ceiling. Chains on his wrists were looped over a hook, and he was just low enough that he could almost stand. The choices were aching shoulder joints, which would eventually dislocate, or the agony of supporting his full body weight on his tiptoes.

I'd already had a bit of a start on him, and his body was a canvas of blues, purples, reds, pinks, and yellows. Some of the marks even had a greenish tint, and there was a large bruise on his chest that reminded me of a nebula. It was quite beautiful.

"I don't know what you think I've done…" the man whispered through his cracked and bleeding lips.

I didn't respond. I walked in and went over to my table of tools. He started to plead then, offering me money, connections… He even offered me his youngest daughter. I grabbed my ear buds off the table and put them in, pulling out my phone and putting on my "Bargain with the Devil" playlist. It seemed like a fitting choice.

Yesterday Toby had been asking his PA how many fingers a person could lose before they bled to death. I put on safety glasses, picked up the handheld saw, and went to work to find out the answer to his question.

The human body never ceased to amaze me. The lack of major arteries let me get through all ten fingers, although the subject passed out before I even made it to the second hand. He was steadily losing blood, but the first wound already seemed to be bleeding less, and I wasn't even sure this would kill him if I left him a few days. Humans were amazingly resilient in some things, and so easily breakable in other ways.

I walked over to my work table, coating my hands and the saw in blue flame to get rid of the blood. I took out my ear buds and paused my music. I supposed it was time to talk to the subject before I sent him on. I liked them to know why.

I walked over and slapped him a few times until he groggily looked at me. The pleading started up right away.

"Please. I'm a husband and a father, and my family—" he started, but I cut him off.

"You beat your wife and children and terrorize them. You would have sold me your youngest daughter. You are even now in negotiations to sell her to a colleague for a more lucrative business deal," I stated.

The man's face contorted. "Then you know who I am. My people will hunt you down and kill you, you piece of shit," he swore. "They're looking for me now—"

I laughed, cutting him off again. Hellbound mortals were always so delusional.

"You think they're looking for you? Do you really? Your wife prays that you will never come home. Your second in command has told everyone that you're on vacation and he's in charge. Your son unfortunately saw me take you from the back of the restaurant where your family was dining, and he went back to the table and told everyone you left to take a phone call. He eventually told his sister the truth, and she wept tears of joy and prayed for your death. That is the legacy you leave behind. No love. No loyalty. Only relief," I told him.

"You lie!" he cried out, his face contorting in rage. "They wouldn't dare!"

"You are not as powerful as you thought, little man. You have killed, raped, beaten, maimed, and destroyed hundreds of lives. There is no redemption for you. Your existence on earth will only lead to more misery and death, and so you have earned a place in hell. I am here to give you passage there. If you think anything that happened here was awful… Just wait until you're dead." I smiled at him then, letting my hellhound nature emerge, and the man shrank back and sputtered in fear.

I let my hands ignite, and I placed them upon his chest, straight over where I saw his blackened, shriveled soul. He screamed as his body ignited in flame.

It was really rather loud and annoying. I sighed, amping up the flame until his vocal cords were burned and I didn't have to hear him. I stepped back and let the fire destroy every trace of the man and cleanse the room. I had the fire engulf me as well, burning away my clothes and all traces of blood. I usually tried to salvage the clothes, but the blood spray from the saw had been more extreme than I expected. Black jeans and black t-shirts were easy enough to replace anyway.

I walked upstairs naked, leaving the lights off. I couldn't help it when my thoughts strayed back to Toby. It would probably be odd to give him an answer to his question. I wasn't sure if there was some way I could casually slip it into conversation. He was probably right that most people didn't talk about torture and death in their routine conversations.

I wouldn't necessarily know. My upbringing had not been… conventional.

As I slipped into the shower, I thought about some way to slip it into conversation anyway. Toby probably wouldn't think it was weird. He did talk about methods of death all the time.

I was pondering how to go about having an actual conversation with Toby, as his friend on the phone had suggested, as I fell into bed, and it was thoughts of Toby that chased me into sleep.

When I was suddenly in a basement room, I knew I was dreaming. I did have some human traits, like the ability to dream. Of course, my dreams were sometimes visions, as well.

I heard a soft whimper and turned around, and I felt my body ignite as I saw Toby cowering on a cot in the corner of the room. He was thinner, his body bruised, his clothes torn and dirty. He was cowering away from me, and I attempted to douse my flame, but then a figure walked through me, and I realized that Toby hadn't been cowering from me—he'd been cowering from this man. I could only see the man's back; he was tall, muscular, and had brown hair. I tried scenting the man, but of course that didn't work in the dream.

Toby's little whimpers of fear nearly broke my heart, but the man just continued to advance on him. A rhythmic banging sound made me look around, but Toby and the man didn't seem to hear it. The man was almost to Toby now, who was trying to make himself as small as possible, and the banging was getting louder and louder…

Which is when I shot up in bed, wide awake.

The sheets were smoldering and a haze of smoke filled the air. Apparently I'd ignited my flame in my sleep because of the dream. The rhythmic banging was also still going, and I realized that hadn't been a part of the dream, but had instead been happening for real. It must have been what woke me, but it stopped in the next moment.

I laid there and contemplated the dream. At least I hoped what I saw was only a dream and not a vision. If it had been a vision, I swore I would circumvent it. No one would take my Toby and do that to him; I would make sure of it. I was a hellhound—I could find anyone I needed to. Perhaps I should mark Toby with my scent somehow, just in case it had been a vision. I ignored the part of me that insisted that would be invasive and that mortals cared about silly things like privacy.

The rhythmic banging started up again, and I shook off my thoughts and climbed out of bed, going over to the window.

Oh. Oh no. Toby was outside on his front porch with a hammer.

I threw on sweatpants and a t-shirt as fast as I could and raced down the stairs. The last time Toby had attempted home improvement there had been quite a bit of blood, and the only thing that had prevented me from rushing over then had been the fact that his friend was there to take care of things. Toby was alone this morning, though. I neither saw nor scented anyone else in the vicinity.

Disaster was imminent.

I flew down the stairs, throwing open my front door. The sound must have alerted Toby, because the banging stopped, thank goodness. I walked onto my own porch, and from the corner of my eye I could see him watching me. I gave a long stretch, letting my t-shirt ride up, and I scented Toby's arousal on the breeze. It was lovely, and I had to concentrate to not have my own cock hardening in response.

I looked over and waved, then hopped off the porch and made my way over to his yard. By the time I made it to his steps, he managed a small wave back.

"Morning," I said, leaning against the railing to the bottom step. I wanted to come onto his porch and snag the hammer out of his hand, but I tried to remember human manners.

"Morning," he said back, then he waved again, only this time it was the hand with the hammer. I did jump up onto the porch then, grabbing it from his hand before he smacked himself in the head with it.

Toby was not the best with tools.

"Uh, thanks," he muttered, turning red.

"No problem. Do you need help with something?" I asked, then I realized I had the perfect opportunity to answer Toby's questions. "I wouldn't want you to lose a finger or something while hammering," I said.

He was staring at me, still embarrassed. "Ugh, you saw the last time Josh was here and we tried fixing my mailbox, didn't you?" he asked, running his hand over his eyes.

I nodded. "All that blood from a wrench," I commented. "And although you wouldn't die from it, I certainly wouldn't want you losing a finger from using a hammer."

That was overkill, wasn't it? Shit. I probably shouldn't bring up losing a finger so many times, but I expected Toby to ask after the first time.

Toby looked at me quizzically. I braced myself for an awkward question, but luckily his curious nature won out.

"You don't think so?" he asked. "I mean, sure, people lose a finger all the time, but probably losing more than one would kill someone."

"There aren't any major arteries in the fingers, so although they might eventually die from blood loss, I think someone could probably lose all their fingers and still survive. Blood clots pretty quickly," I answered.

Toby had a thoughtful expression on his face. "Hmm. Maybe a whole hand then? Surely if they lost the whole hand they'd die?"

"If no medical treatment was received and no tourniquet was applied, then yes. But with some care someone could survive that as well," I answered.

"Oh yeah, there was that hiker that cut off his arm when it was stuck in a boulder, and he lived. I saw the movie," Toby said thoughtfully. "Although I think it was stuck above him and didn't have blood flow anymore."

"Yes," I added. "If the victim had their arms below the heart line, and nothing was done to stem the flow of blood, then amputating an arm would result in enough blood loss to die if steps were not taken to stem the blood flow."

I had once cut off a hellbound mortal's arm. I'd gotten through both before he died.

"You could probably cut off both arms before someone bled out," I added helpfully. "Although I think one would do it. But a person could live with all ten fingers cut off."

Toby got an odd look on his face then.

Shit. That was weird, wasn't it. Probably too much information.

CHAPTER 3

TOBY

One of my current projects features a supernatural witch—Josh was right that I was doing something paranormal—so I thought maybe I could have him be tortured and he could magically stop the flow of blood. My poor main character. Readers were going to feel so bad for him. It was gonna be fantastic.

I realized then that I hadn't said anything, and my neighbor was staring at me.

Dammit. I was totally being weird again, getting lost in book ideas. Josh would so yell at me if he were here.

"I'm a writer," I explained, like that made everything better. "I'm not, like, a serial killer or anything," I laughed.

Hot neighbor was still just looking at me.

"Or a stalker. Not a serial killer or a stalker," I added. Then I could have hit myself in the head. God, could I be any more awkward?

"I'm Toby," I said, sticking out my hand, because I figured if we talked about dismemberment together I ought to at least introduce myself.

"Dex," he said, reaching his hand out and enfolding mine within it.

Fuck. He had very large hands. Like his hand just totally wrapped mine up in it, and I was getting horny wondering if my hot neighbor, aka Dex, was that big everywhere. Because yes please.

And he totally did have tattoos peaking out from underneath his t-shirt. They looked like symbols of some sort. I realized I was just staring at him, our hands clasped together, and I pulled mine back.

"Do you mow your own lawn?" I blurted out.

Dammit. I really needed to get out more. I was so out of practice at having normal conversations.

"I do. Do you need yours mowed as well?" Dex asked, smiling a little.

Ohmygod. Yes please. I tried not to blush just thinking about it.

"Um, I usually hire someone," I muttered. Because yeah, yard work was not my thing. Tools were not my thing, as evidenced by the fact that I'd almost brained myself with my own hammer.

Which reminded me that sexy, muscular guys were not usually my thing either, as much as I would like them to be. I was a writer who didn't get enough exercise or sun and liked potato chips too much. And I was socially awkward. I mean, we'd just had a whole conversation about severing body parts.

"So how do you know so much about dismemberment?" I asked.

I almost facepalmed myself. Great pick up line, Toby. And if he was a serial killer, that probably wasn't a good thing to ask either, although my brain seemed to have decided he wasn't since he saved me from hammering myself.

This time Dex looked a little awkward. "Um, I have some experience in traumatic injuries," he murmured.

Huh. That was weirdly vague.

"Like, you're a doctor?" I asked.

"I have a lot of medical knowledge," he answered, which wasn't really an answer.

So he wasn't a doctor, but he had medical knowledge and experience in "traumatic injuries"—maybe he really was a serial killer? Although Josh would still insist he was something normal like a nurse or an EMT.

Ohh, maybe he had been in the military and was one of those soldiers who worked in interrogation. That probably happened in real life and not just the movies, right? They'd totally cut off limbs and stuff, wouldn't they?

"Are you in the service? Were you, like, an interrogator or some-thing?" I asked, because my mouth didn't always have a mute button.

Dex looked vaguely uncomfortable. "I, uh… I've served…"

"It's ok," I said, patting his arm. "You don't have to talk about it. I'm sorry if my questions brought back bad memories."

"It's ok. I don't mind questions," he said, looking at my hand, which had stopped patting his arm and was now sort of rubbing it, because the man had some gorgeous forearms. I didn't even know forearms were my thing, but his were lean and corded with muscle and hairy, and he felt really warm.

I forced myself to pull my hand away, chuckling nervously. "Good! I sometimes get lost in my head plotting, and some of my books are fluffy and sweet, but some are thrillers, and there's the occasional bad guy. There's also the occasional good guy who's badass, because that's so totally hot, so, yeah, dismemberment and stuff," I finished lamely.

"Well, anytime you have any questions for your books, feel free to ask," Dex said. "I'm happy to help."

It almost looked like his eyes glowed for a second, but when I blinked, he was just my normal, although excessively hot, neighbor.

I chuckled nervously again. "Ok! Well, I'm gonna go write about hot men while I'm feeling inspired by you. I mean, your answers, of course. Yeah."

With that I turned around, opened my door, gave an awkward little wave again, and shut the door behind me. My god, I really needed to get out and do more peopling. I was totally an embarrassment to my-self.

I waited to hear his footsteps leave my porch, and after a moment I heard him going down the steps.

"You're such an idiot, Toby," I muttered to myself. "You should not be talking about cutting off body parts with the hot neighbor."

I thought I heard a laugh, but when I peeked out the curtain at the front window, my neighbor was far enough away that there was no way he'd heard me.

I sighed and then headed over to the couch to grab my laptop, where I'd left it when I'd decided I needed to go and try to fix the num-bers on the front of the house, which were attached a little crookedly. It was amazing the things I could accomplish when I was procrastinating.

My house was clean, I'd done some laundry, and I'd even resorted to home improvement projects, all because I really needed to write my next chapter.

Hot Neighbor had definitely provided some inspiration, though, and I opened up my current work in progress and got writing. If the badass vampire love interest suddenly started to resemble my neighbor… Well, I was fairly confident Dex wouldn't be reading my books. I started typing away, losing myself in my paranormal world.

By the time I came up for air, the sun was setting, my stomach was growling, and my whole body felt stiff. I closed my computer and wandered into the kitchen, opening the fridge. There was nothing good to eat. I closed it and opened the freezer. Frozen vegetables and frozen meat that I'd cook someday. Maybe. I checked the pantry. Still some chips left, and I took off the chip clip and munched on them as I opened the fridge again.

Because, you know, maybe something had magically appeared in the thirty seconds since I'd last checked.

Nope. Fridge was still sadly devoid of anything resembling a meal.

I sighed, picking up my phone to take a look at what was available on the food delivery app, only I got mildly distracted by the little red circle with the number of unread emails listed. I hated when it got into the double digits. I may not be able to stock my fridge, but by god I could keep my inbox cleared out.

I clicked my email and deleted half the messages—sales, store updates, and some random health newsletter I swear I never signed up for. I totally didn't think beet juice was the miracle cure for all my ailments. Oh, one of my author friends had a new newsletter out. That would be fun to look at.

Then I saw a random email to my author account. Sometimes fan emails were awesome, but sometimes it was someone critiquing my work or telling me something was wrong, and I wasn't sure if I was in the mood for that tonight. I put the chips down and sat down at the kitchen table, debating leaving it for tomorrow. Of course, the suspense would probably keep me up all night if I didn't open it.

Once I clicked on it, I skimmed it over, wincing a bit the further I got. I went back and read it a second time, even though I felt nauseous.

Fuck. This was from a "fan" who had caused me some issues, and I'd thought removing him from everything and blocking him had taken care of the issue.

Apparently not.

The guy had started off after my first book as a fan—he'd been in my Facebook group and followed all my socials. Then the messages had started. They'd been ok at first, if a little presumptuous. He'd told me stuff that was wrong with my book, like that my characters shouldn't have done this or that, and did I know I'd gotten some aspect of mythology wrong in my book?

It was slightly infuriating—like, dude, I write fiction. I could make up whatever I wanted to. That was what made writing so awesome. If I wanted Medusa to be a guy who had a bad hairdresser experience, then that was totally my prerogative. But I'd taken the advice of my PA and just replied with a simple "Thanks for the feedback! I'm glad you enjoyed my book!"

Only apparently that wasn't enough for this guy, because he'd gotten more and more hostile, eventually critiquing my sex scenes and asking me when the last time I'd had anything up my ass had been. That was the point at which I'd blocked him from all socials.

He'd sent me an angry email—he was my biggest fan, and how could I do that to him, and blah blah blah. So I'd blocked his email, and I had figured that would be the end of it. I wrote under a pen name, and no one knew my real name, where I lived, or how to get in touch with me. Sometimes people sucked on the internet, and I thought this guy was just an example of that. I'd almost been ready for him to blast me in other groups or post bad reviews, and I'd been relieved when I hadn't heard anything.

Apparently my relief was premature.

This email was the most toxic so far. He made some long comparison about how he was like one MC in my book and I was like another. It scared me a little that he compared himself to the slightly unhinged MC who kidnapped the other MC. Of course it all worked out in my book and they fell madly in love, but that was because it was fiction.

Stalking and kidnapping in real life were totally not sexy. I didn't think I needed to put that disclaimer on my books, but maybe I should start? Like "Hey folks! Please don't try this at home! Consent is important!"

I was spiraling, and maybe hyperventilating a little bit. I focused on trying to calm down my breathing.

He was just a rabid fan. He didn't know where I lived. I kept my address private and had everything sent to a PO box. He wasn't actually stalking me—one crazy email did not equal a stalker like I wrote about. Josh was always telling me I blew stuff out of proportion, and I'm sure I was doing that here. This guy was just creepy as fuck and had to have the last word.

I just really hoped this was the last word from him.

Chapter 4

Dexter

I stared at the hammer on the table by my front door. I knew Toby was up—I'd seen lights and heard his footsteps, but he hadn't had coffee and breakfast delivered this morning.

Would it be weird to return his hammer and bring him some coffee?

I wished I knew more about humans, aside from how breakable they were.

I usually didn't mind that I was so disconnected from the human world. My parents were good people, but they were first generation hellhounds that were content with just each other. We were constantly moving around hunting evil, and I felt like a third wheel more often than not. It wasn't until I'd almost reached maturity that I'd been given to Wilder to raise, and that was when I'd finally found my pack and where I belonged. We weren't a conventional group—I suppose hellhounds never were—so I never really bridged the gap between me and humanity.

Not everyone in my pack was so awkward with humans, however. If Jude were here, he'd know exactly what to say and how to talk to Toby. Jude had grown up thinking he was human, and he knew the most about the human world.

I supposed I could call and ask him. My pack was scattered right now, all of us in different areas taking care of sending hopeless souls on to the afterlife before they could do more damage on the mortal plane. We hadn't had a central location to call home since we'd had to leave Wilder's last compound. Humans tended to notice when you didn't age, and it had probably been a decade since we'd all had a home base. We were constantly on the lookout for one, but no place had felt quite right to any of us.

Paradise Falls felt weirdly welcoming, though. When I'd first pulled into town, a sense of rightness had filled me, and I'd immediately looked into buying a house.

Then I'd seen a demon in town. Then another demon. Then an angel. So many afterlifers in one area usually spelled trouble, and hell-hounds generally tried to avoid afterlifers since the first gen had left hell for the mortal plane.

Only… None of them had paid me any attention at all.

Then I'd felt the vague miasma of evil, only my hellhound hadn't sensed mortality behind it. I'd almost packed up and left at that point, but I'd already started to become… attached to my interesting little neighbor. And I could tell that the evil floating around town wasn't normal at all.

When the coffee shop owner, who was apparently an oracle, had texted me about a demon, I'd had the urge to get involved. Luckily that had been resolved satisfactorily. I still chuckled to think that the rogue demon had thought he could order me around. He'd certainly found out differently.

Ah, how satisfying those few days had been.

At any rate, once that was dealt with, Paradise Falls had gone back to its homey, welcoming feeling, and I had begun to think that may-be this town could be something of a home base. There was a quaint downtown, but there were ample rural areas as well—Paradise Falls was actually quite large. It was within a two hour drive of two major cities, giving us plenty of areas to hunt evil, and I hadn't sensed any other hellhounds in either city. It wasn't that we wouldn't get along with another pack—but if there were hellhounds hunting in this area, then it wouldn't need us.

On top of all that, the sprawling house I was in was large enough for a few of us—it had four bedrooms and was on a large piece of property. It had neighbors on both sides, although Toby was much closer to me than the old lady on the other side. I also knew she would probably be glad to sell, and her property was up against a protected open space. The three houses, including Toby's, were kind of out in the middle of nowhere, and they would be perfect for our pack.

I hadn't mentioned it, however, because I didn't want Toby to move, and if we all lived here he would probably notice something weird. Although Toby lived in his own world most of the time, so maybe he wouldn't.

I also kind of wanted to keep Toby to myself. There was just something about the human…

Which brought me back to my current dilemma. Was bringing over coffee and returning his hammer weird? What did humans do when they wanted to get to know each other?

I sighed and walked into the kitchen, grabbing my cell phone to make a call.

"Hey, Jude," I said when he picked up, then I almost banged my head against the counter.

"Dex! What's up? Don't make it bad!" he laughed.

Jude had chosen his name because he was an avid Beatles fan, and somehow he never got tired of the jokes. The rest of us, however…

I sighed again before replying, and Jude got serious at the sound. "Hey, all ok there? Trouble in Paradise Falls?"

"No. Paradise Falls is actually really nice. There was a bit of an issue with a demon, but it was handled by an angel and an oracle, and I helped a bit," I replied.

Jude hummed thoughtfully. "'Really nice'? I don't think I've ever heard you refer to a town as 'really nice' before. Where are you staying?"

"I, uh, bought a house," I admitted.

Shit. This wasn't where I was planning on taking the conversation.

"Really?" Jude questioned. "You never purchase property."

"That wasn't why I called," I said, hoping to cut that line of questioning off. Yes, I thought Paradise Falls might work, but I had to figure out Toby before my pack descended on the town.

"Ah, ok. So what's up, brother?" Jude asked.

I rubbed the back of my neck, feeling vaguely stupid. Now that it came down to it, I wasn't quite sure what to say. "Uh… So… You grew up among humans," I stated.

"Yep," Jude answered.

"So you know how to talk to them, and you know what would be considered normal," I stated.

"Are the humans there giving you issues?" Jude growled, as if I couldn't take care of myself. I almost rolled my eyes.

"No, of course not. It's just that, well, I have this neighbor…" I started, then I cleared my throat, unsure where to go from there.

Jude laughed. "Ah, Dex, are you asking me about dating humans?"

"No!" I answered. I then added, "Maybe?"

"You trying to figure out how to talk to your cute neighbor?" Jude asked, still chuckling.

"How do you know he's cute?" I asked suspiciously.

"Because you're calling me looking for advice on how to talk to humans," Jude answered reasonably. "Obviously you think he's cute. So what do you need to know, Dex?"

"I have his hammer. He didn't get coffee delivery this morning, and he usually does. Would it be normal to bring his hammer over and a cup of coffee for him?" I asked.

"Well of course you should return the hammer. That's totally normal. Not sure on the coffee, though. It might come off as a little stalkerish to admit you know when he gets coffee delivered and when he doesn't. Or to give him coffee how he likes it prepared, which I'm sure you know with your attention to detail."

"I should give him coffee that isn't prepared to his liking?" I asked. "That seems strange."

"No, maybe just skip the coffee altogether is what I'm saying," Jude replied. "You don't want to come off like a stalker."

"He doesn't think I'm a stalker. He thinks I'm a serial killer," I answered reasonably.

Jude must have been taking a drink, because I heard the sound of him spitting something out and then coughing. "He thinks what?" he gasped.

"That I'm a serial killer," I answered again. "I heard him telling his friend on the phone."

"Why the hell does he think that?" Jude asked once he stopped coughing.

"Well, he was inquiring about death from stomach wounds. So obviously, I was helpful," I explained.

"Obviously, he was helpful," Jude muttered under his breath. "Ok, listen, Dex, you can't talk about death and dismemberment with humans."

"Why not?" I asked. "He brought it up. I might have brought up losing fingers, but only because he was asking about that."

"Dex," Jude sighed out. I could tell he was probably rubbing his forehead. He did that sometimes when our interactions with humans didn't meet his standards.

"And anyway, I think now he thinks I used to torture people for the military, not that I'm a serial killer," I added helpfully.

"Ok," Jude said, "obviously I'm missing something here, because it isn't normal for humans to ask those sort of questions unless they're serial killers."

"Oh, he isn't a serial killer, although he has admitted that maybe he's a stalker," I replied.

Jude sputtered through the phone, so I added proudly, "But don't worry, he's only stalking me."

I could hear Jude doing some deep breathing then. I gave him a minute, going over to the coffee machine and starting a cup. He had said not to bring a cup for Toby, but maybe if I had my own cup of coffee with me I could offer some to him. That would be polite, right?

"I think you better start at the beginning," Jude finally said.

So I told him about Toby, his writing, and the conversations I'd listened in on with his friends and personal assistant. I might have left out some of the details—he didn't need to know how hot Toby thought I was, or how cute I thought he was—but I explained the basics.

"Ok," Jude finally answered. "I guess that makes a little more sense. He isn't actually stalking you. He thinks you're hot. Although it kind of sounds like you're stalking him if you're listening in on his phone conversations and keeping track of his delivery schedule."

"He's cute," I said.

"Hmm. Well, then I guess there's only one answer." Then Jude started singing, "Let him into your heart, and then you can start to make it better."

"Jude," I said, rubbing my own forehead now.

"You have found him, now go and get him," Jude sang.

"Jude, seriously," I cut in.

"Remember to let him under your skin, then you'll begin to make it better better better…" Jude continued to sing.

"Jude!" I half yelled, cutting him off.

He only chuckled.

"I never got that anyway. How would I let him under my skin? Am I supposed to flay myself and drape him in it? I don't think most humans would enjoy that," I mused.

Jude sighed then. "Man, this is gonna be hopeless. Look, just return the hammer, and just try to… I don't know… Be normal. Don't talk about flaying people or dismemberment or let him know that you know when he gets coffee delivery."

"I thought it was a fool who played it cool," I smirked.

Jude laughed. "Hey, no using lyrics against me."

"You're the one who chose a Beatles song for a name," I answered.

"Better than choosing the name of a serial killer from tv," he responded.

"That was a good show!" I protested. "What I watched of it, anyway. A serial killer with a moral code. Seemed like the perfect name to me." So I'd only seen a few episodes of my namesake television show, but I had grown rather fond of the name.

"Listen though, about the town…" Jude started.

"I don't know," I cut in. "Maybe. It feels good here. But I'm not ready for the whole pack to descend just yet."

"Because of your cute neighbor?" Jude asked.

"He feels like pack to my hellhound," I answered quietly.

"Ok. Well, keep me posted. And just… I don't know… try to act like a normal human," Jude said before we said our farewells and hung up.

Yeah. If only it were that simple. If I knew what acting like a normal human entailed, I wouldn't have called Jude to begin with.

I supposed he at least answered the coffee question. Sort of. I debated bringing the cup I'd made for myself over then decided against it since I hadn't asked Jude. I'd just bring the hammer over, and Toby and

I would have a normal, human conversation.
Yep. It should be easy.

Chapter 5

I had managed to eat myself into a chip coma last night and mostly ignore the disturbing email. In the light of day, it all seemed kind of silly anyway. Writers got advice and weird opinions from people all the time. People said things online they didn't mean and would never say in real life.

Yup. I was hoping that was the case and that I never heard from the creep again.

I'd probably tell my PA at some point, but right now I was in the zone. I had a couple thousand words done this morning already, but I was currently in the hot vampire's point of view. He had walked in on a bit of a blood bath, but I didn't actually want the main character dead. If the walls were painted with his blood, would he still be alive? I mean, sure, I could use magic to explain a lot of stuff, but I didn't want to be totally unrealistic.

The doorbell rang, and I took my computer with me to the front door, pondering the scene I was writing. I remembered at the last moment to look out the peephole before opening the door.

Ah, Serial Killer Neighbor was here. Perfect.

I opened the door, asking, "How much blood can a person lose before they die?"

"Depends on the human's size," he responded.

I motioned him in, saying, "My guy is average height and weight."

"Hmm. Probably about 85 ounces before death. Although the human would probably pass out around 65 ounces or so. They'd be cool and clammy and pale looking at that point as well," he added.

I looked at him, vaguely disgruntled. He must have noticed, because he stopped, looking a bit awkward. Gah, even awkward looked sexy on him. So unfair.

"Listen, ounces mean nothing to me," I said. "Are we talking enough to spray the walls and have pools of blood on the ground? Or is that much blood everywhere unrealistic?" I asked, sitting at my kitchen table and starting to type again.

"Oh," he laughed, sounding relieved, although I didn't know why. "Yeah, 65 ounces is about a half a gallon. So think about if you took a half a gallon of milk and threw it onto the walls a cup at a time. If it was a small room, you'd have more than enough to have a coating on the three walls, and it would naturally drip down and pool on the ground. That's assuming there were numerous injuries that sprayed blood, of course."

"Of course," I answered, adding that description to my writing. I stopped then, looking up at him. "Three walls?" I asked.

"Well, yeah, because I assume whoever was making the human bleed would be standing in front of the fourth wall, so that area would not be as blood coated. Although the person who did the torturing would definitely be coated in blood. Of course if it was one major injury to make the human bleed out you wouldn't have blood everywhere. There would be a focused spray," he said.

"An evil vampire is doing the torturing," I said absently, still typing. "But yeah, I don't want a focused spray. This is extended torture, so I'm going with lots of smaller wounds," I mumbled.

"Of course, not all wounds spray. They're just as likely to drip as to splatter," he added helpfully.

"Shit," I said. I hadn't thought of that. "I really wanted blood on the walls when the vampire love interest comes in."

"Well, with so much blood pooling on the ground, and so much blood obviously on the human—" he started.

"Witch," I interrupted.

"—on the witch, then," he went on, "I'd think the bad guy could easily smear blood on the walls with his hands. Or even kick it up with his feet. Vampires are supposed to like blood, aren't they? I'd think an evil one would enjoy getting messy."

"Oh, yeah, perfect," I responded, my fingers flying. "Help yourself to coffee or whatever," I mumbled vaguely. I knew it was probably rude, but he had just given me a great idea, and I had to get it down.

I wasn't sure how much time had passed when I finished my scene, but I looked up and Serial Killer Neighbor—Dex, I mean (I really had to stop calling him Serial Killer Neighbor in my head)—was sitting at my kitchen island and drinking a cup of coffee. There was another cup across from him, and my hammer was laying on the island next to him.

Ah, that must have been why he stopped over.

I blushed then. Shit. I was the worst host ever. How long had I made Dex sit and wait for me?

"Ah, sorry. I was just in the middle of a scene, and sometimes I get a little lost in my head, and—" I started.

"It's fine," he smiled.

God, he was sexy when he smiled. I got up and walked over to the island, trying to be casual as I leaned against it next to him.

"You're cute when you're absorbed," he added.

Fuck. I might die of a heart attack right here in my kitchen. My sexy, possibly-serial-killer neighbor thought I was cute? Fuck.

"Ah, ok. Thanks. Cute is good. Yeah. Good. Cute. Uh, anyway, you must have come to return my hammer, right?" I mumbled, walking over and picking up the hammer. "Because I left it with you. Or actually, you took it from me. Not in a bad way! I mean, to, like, stop me from hurting myself. Not that I do that. Hurt myself, I mean. Not on purpose, but you know power tools," I babbled.

Fuck. Brain to mouth emergency. Emergency alert. STOP TALKING!

Only brain or mouth didn't get the memo, because I picked up the hammer and added, "Although a hammer isn't really a power tool, but it's a tool, and yeah, me and tools, we don't play nicely."

I might have been gesticulating with the hammer in my hand, because suddenly Sexy Neighbor was up and had grabbed my hand right before I managed to smack myself with the hammer.

I chuckled weakly, muttering, "Case in point."

Only then I was distracted, because somehow Sexy Neighbor's body was really close to mine, almost caging me in against the kitchen island, and his hand was on my hand, and I could feel the heat coming off of him.

"You're really hot," I mumbled. "Oh god! I mean, like, temperature hot! You're really temperature hot. Not that I'm saying you're ugly or anything! Because of course you're hot appearance wise too. I mean…"

Fuck! I groaned and closed my eyes, although Sexy Neighbor looked more amused than anything else, and his hand was still on mine, and his skin was really warm, and it was making my whole body warm, but in a really good way, and if he moved any closer, he was going to know exactly how good he was making feel.

I opened one eye, and yup, he was still there, and he still looked mildly amused, although he took a deep breath in then, like he was gonna say something, only his eyes widened and suddenly he didn't look so amused. He looked… double fuck—he looked intense.

"Are you gonna kiss me?" I asked, because brain to mouth filter was still apparently broken, and he totally looked like he might kiss me, although maybe that was my brain running away into fantasy land again.

"Would that be acceptable?" he murmured, and yes his face was definitely closer to mine, and he was inhaling deeply, almost like he was smelling me, only instead of being creepy, it was insanely hot.

"Yeah. Yes. Totally acceptable. Definitely acceptable," I muttered.

Then I was cut off, because his lips pressed against mine. His hand must have taken the hammer from me and put it down, because my hands were free to wrap around his back, and one of his hands was in my hair, pulling my head back for a better angle. The kiss started gentle, and then he licked at my lips and I opened my mouth to him. His tongue slid inside, and god, he tasted like campfire and spices. I groaned as our tongues tangled together, and he pulled back slightly to nip at my bottom lip.

I pressed my body against his, and he was hard everywhere, and fuck if I didn't moan again. I tried really hard not to hump against him as his mouth ravished mine. It was pure bliss—tongues and lips and teeth occasionally nibbling—and when he pulled back, I was breathing heavily and barely able to hold myself up.

"Fuck, you're a good kisser. That's totally going into my scene," I mumbled.

Then my eyes shot open, mortified.

Luckily, Sexy Neighbor just chuckled.

"I'd be happy to provide inspiration for any of the scenes you need to write," he murmured.

With that, he gave me a soft peck on the lips, smiled at me, and turned and walked out of the kitchen. I heard my front door close behind him.

"Holy shit," I mumbled. Was I in a coma? A fever induced dream? In what universe did a sexy neighbor come in, tell you everything you needed to know to complete your current chapter, then kiss you senseless?

Damn, I was horny. I was also incredibly inspired. I adjusted myself then sat back down at the table, ready to write a really fantastic kissing scene between my two MCs.

By the time I finished my sexy scene and came up for air, reality hit me.

Sexy Neighbor had kissed me.

I hadn't imagined that, right? It had actually happened? And then he had just… walked out. Like it was perfectly normal to randomly kiss your neighbor.

What was I supposed to do now? Would there be more kissing? Because, yes, please. Was I supposed to call him or something? Or stop over at his house? Could I pretend I needed to borrow a cup of sugar? Was that way too 1950s?

My god, I was so bad at dating. Not that this was dating, because I'm sure Sexy Neighbor wouldn't be interested in dating a reclusive writer who was awkward at best. But if this was hooking up, I was bad at that too. I mean, yeah, I'd done some random hookups in college, but most of those involved parties and alcohol and very little actual conversation. Plus, I had the benefit of knowing I probably wouldn't run into those guys again if I made a complete fool of myself. That was totally not the case with Sexy Neighbor. I'd have to see him everyday.

Fuck.

I grabbed my phone and texted Josh and Sebbie. This definitely required a night of gossiping and drinking.

Chapter 6

Dexter

I was driving around the outskirts of the city that was about an hour away from Paradise Falls, hunting down the faint tinge of evil on the air. After kissing Toby, my hellhound had been itchy as hell. It had been hard to walk away from him, but as much as I'd wanted to take him up against his kitchen island, I wanted more from him.

I'd had sex with humans before, but Toby was special. I had the urge to woo him.

I chuckled to myself thinking about what Jude would say if I asked about giving a human the corpses of his enemies as a courting gift. Not that Toby had any enemies; he was all sweetness and light, his soul shining brightly, not a speck of rot on it.

I hadn't even really meant to kiss him, but I'd smelled his arousal, and I hadn't been able to help myself. He was so tempting.

I tried to clear my thoughts of Toby to focus on the hunt. I was in a very wealthy suburb outside the city, where the mansions had a lot of property and were gated, but electronics wouldn't stop me. I could feel the pull of a rotten soul, and I followed it until I reached one particularly large property. It was covered in a miasma of evil, and I knew there was at least one hellbound mortal inside.

I noted cameras as I drove by, so I didn't stop. My features would never appear clearly on camera, but my car would, so I parked about a mile away, grabbed my working bag, and walked the rest of the way back to the mansion. As I got closer, I could smell the rot and decay of the human soul getting stronger, a symptom of a soul too far gone for redemption in this lifetime.

I contemplated bringing the human back home to take my time with them, but it was only afternoon, and the possibility of people being about made that more difficult. It was probably best to dispose of them here. I had some tools with me, and I'd be able to have at least a few hours of fun.

I scaled the wall, avoiding the cameras easily. Once inside the property, I sensed the dogs. They were approaching quickly, but at least they were silent so far. What an added bonus. I loved dogs.

They ran up growling, probably ready to start barking an alert, but the moment they saw me, they fell to their stomachs and started whining.

"Oh, what cute boys you are!" I murmured, crouching down and motioning them forward. "Are you good boys? I bet you are!" I said as they belly crawled toward me, tails wagging at my voice.

They were large German shepherds, and they were obviously well trained. I had no doubt that they would find a home after their owner was disposed of. Guard dogs like these went for a small fortune.

"You didn't know you were protecting an evil human, did you? You're just doing your job, aren't you?" I murmured as I scratched them both. One rolled over for me to pet his belly, so I gave him a nice rub.

Eventually I stood up. "Alright boys, I have work to do. Where's your owner?"

They stood as well, obviously realizing playtime was over, and trotted along beside me, tails wagging and tongues lolling. I patted them occasionally as I walked, but I knew I'd have to make sure to leave them outside. Dogs who licked up blood at crime scenes didn't tend to get adopted. Humans were weird about things like that. I gave a mental shrug as the dogs led me around a beautiful built-in pool to a patio and sliding glass doors.

I smiled as I saw the electronic keypad on the outside of the door. It was obviously hooked to the house alarm system as well, which made things even easier. I placed my hand on it, allowing some flame to wind its way down through the wires. The dogs whined a bit at the surge of hellhound power, but I just made a reassuring sound and they hushed right up. What good boys.

I wondered idly if Toby liked dogs. I bet he did. He totally seemed like a dog person. I could just imagine him curled up on his sofa with a dog next to him while he wrote. Although Toby was a bit absent mind-ed, and I wasn't sure he'd remember to feed them. Of course, if Toby lived with me, I'd make sure the dogs were fed and exercised. Although maybe I was getting a bit ahead of myself with that thought.

With a blink the light on the keypad went out, and I listened for a moment to see if a phone rang. I'd used enough flame to disable the device but not fully put it offline, because these companies had fail safes built in for losing contact completely.

Modern day technologies had made things more difficult, but we had all practiced disabling alarm systems at Wilder's compound. They hadn't been so advanced that many years ago, but it was enough of a start for us all to figure it out. It was amazing what hellhound fire could accomplish. There was no doubt it was a bit miraculous, and we made the most of it.

There was still a regular lock, but that was easy enough to burn through, and I slid open the glass door noiselessly. The dogs whined a bit when I put my hand up for them to stay, but they obeyed, and I shut the door behind me. I was in an opulent bar room that was obviously meant to be used with the pool and the outdoor area. Thankfully, it was empty.

It was mid afternoon, but I only sensed three souls in the house. One was my rotten hell-bound mortal, and then there was a soul that was… slightly rancid. It wasn't enough to justify my presence, but if that mortal continued down their current path, there was a good chance they'd get a visit from a hellhound.

The last soul was… I sniffed the air, letting my hellhound out. Underneath the rot and decay, there was a fresh smell, like an ocean breeze, only there was a faintly acrid scent to it. A true innocent, then, but there was an underlying sense of fear or worry. Hells, I hoped it wasn't a little kid.

I let out a growl at the very thought, and I must have been heard, because a feminine voice called out, "Marcus, did you let the dogs in the house?"

Whoever Marcus was, he must not have heard, and I could hear the female walking this way. She was the slightly rancid soul. I moved over and out of sight, leaving my bag on the ground next to me—there was no need to have her screaming when she saw me. I would deal with her before I had my fun with this Marcus.

"Marcus?" she asked, stepping into the room, and I came out behind her and put my hand over her mouth.

"Scream and I'll snap your neck," I growled as she began to struggle.

She stilled at that, and I heard muffled talking against my hand. I let it loosen slightly but kept it in position.

"I don't know anything," she whispered. "Please, just let me go."

Ah, the smell of deceit. I turned her around and pinned her against the wall. I knew my eyes were glowing, my face beginning to change shape. It would be enough to make me unrecognizable. Fire burst up on my back, and I let it slowly engulf my shirt.

"You know enough. Your soul reeks of decay," I snarled.

"What…" she whispered, eyes wide.

"Lucky for you, I'm not here for you. Not yet. Keep on this path, though, and one of my kind will come for you next. Do you understand?" I bit out.

Her eyes remained wide and glassy, and I could feel her quivering in my hands. I gave her a shake, asking again, "Do you understand?"

"Yes! Yes, I understand," she whimpered.

"I'm going to let you go now, and you're going to get in your car and drive as far away as you can, or else I'm going to find you. You won't like what happens if I find you," I growled.

"Yes, ok. I'll go. Please, just let me go," she pleaded.

I sighed, then I did just that. She backed out of the room, her eyes on me, and I walked over to pick up my bag. By the time I did that, she had turned around and was running. I followed behind her, because it wouldn't do to have her warn Marcus, but she ran through a front hall, grabbing keys off a table and rushing out the front door. I could see through the entryway as she climbed into the tiny sports car in the wide, circular driveway and squealed off into the afternoon.

I had read enough off of her soul to know that she wouldn't be going to the cops. She and her husband were up to their eyeballs in illegal activities, and she was also cheating on him. My guess was that she would run to her lover for back-up. Maybe she'd even be glad that Marcus was dead.

I didn't have much hope for her fixing her ways, but that was up to her. Perhaps I'd leave her a nice blood bath to come home to. Maybe that would drive the message home, although I hated to leave the body behind. It always caused such issues. Still, if I went the bloody route, I could let Toby know which cuts were most likely to spray versus drip…

But I was getting sidetracked.

I let my hellhound form go so that I looked like a normal human again. A shirtless human, but oh well. Marcus would have other things to worry about aside from my lack of a shirt.

I followed the smell of rot to a set of stairs. Luckily, the innocent soul smelled like it was in the opposite direction. I stalked upstairs and down a hallway, passing by bedrooms until I found a closed door. I tried the handle, but it was locked. It was easy enough to burn the lock away and gently ease the door open.

Marcus was sitting in a plush office chair with headphones on and nothing else. He was stroking himself and watching something on his screen. Without even touching him, I could see some of the heinous acts he'd committed to have such a blackened soul. Looks like I'd be burning his computer and all his files when I was done with him— Marcus liked to make raunchy videos with unwilling participants. I'd have to see if Liam could hack into his accounts and delete anything this guy had in the storm or the fog or whatever the fuck people called internet storage. Technology was obviously not my thing, but Liam was pretty good with it.

I took in the room. The office was a good size, not too big. I figured I'd be able to test out the blood splatter idea quite well in here. I'm sure Toby would like to know if his idea would work out for his book.

With a grin, I let my bag of tools drop loudly enough for Marcus to startle and look over.

Time to have some fun.

I let my flame burn the blood off my bare skin and let it lightly lick over the surfaces in the office, removing any traces I might have left in the room. I'd already fried the computer and anything else electronic, and I'd sent a text to Liam with the guy's passwords and stuff, which he'd been all too willing to tell me once we'd been underway.

I contemplated the corpse in front of me. What a disappointment.

I'd never thought too much about it, but the problem with blood spray was that you were usually hitting an artery, and the human was likely to bleed out much more quickly. To really get maximum blood everywhere, you'd have to hit a lot of arteries at once, which was really not very satisfying. Death would be very fast with that much speedy blood loss. Cuts that bled out more slowly just didn't splatter, though, although they did form satisfying puddles.

Well, they would on a bare floor, anyway. Marcus's office was unfortunately carpeted, so it ended up as a saturated, bloody carpet. Still, there had been enough blood for some to pool on the carpet.

I'd have to make sure Toby hadn't set his scene in a carpeted room. Shag carpet especially would probably soak up quite a bit of blood.

I looked out the window. Dusk had fallen outside, and I supposed I needed to decide whether I was going to dispose of Marcus or not. As satisfying as it would be to leave Marcus for the woman to find, the innocent human might just as easily find the body. Plus, then there would be police and questions and all that stuff, and I hated wasting all those human resources on a crime they would never solve.

Missing persons were always easier than murder scenes.

A house fire would nicely take care of his body and the bloody remains, and I kind of didn't want the wife to have the house—she didn't deserve it. But that meant I would need to deal with the innocent human.

I'd kept tabs on the person, and despite Marcus getting quite vocal at the end there, the human had not moved from their location in the house. I sighed. I supposed I would have to retrieve them. It would have been easier if they'd just run off like the wife had.

I didn't think it was a child. The woman and Marcus had given no indication of corrupting children in their darkened souls, and I hadn't sensed any offspring. Although really, if it was a teenager, I could see those two not feeling very parental. Marcus and the woman were both monsters.

I left my pants on—not too much blood splatter on them, and the blood that was on them blended in because they were black. My skin was clean, and I grabbed my to-go bag and followed the scent to the mortal.

I took the staircase downstairs and ended up at a door on the main floor. After burning through the lock, I found a set of steps leading down another level. I followed those down into a wine cellar. I almost stopped and grabbed a few bottles—I knew Toby liked wine—but I was starting to get a sense of urgency about the innocent mortal.

I didn't think living in a wine cellar was normal human behavior.

I wound my way through the wine racks and found myself at another door hidden at the back of the cellar. It was also locked, and it occurred to me for the first time that the lock to come downstairs had been on the outside of the door, not the inside.

Whoever was down here was being held captive.

I burned through the lock and slowly opened the door. I didn't see anyone at first, then a form came charging out at me, all scratching nails and yelling and flailing limbs.

"Shit!" I cried out, grabbing ahold of the arms that were currently trying to pummel me and scrape my skin off.

"Let me go you fucking asshole!" a man's voice cried out, and his legs continued to kick at me as he struggled.

I was trying not to hurt him, but he was a wiggly fucker. I spied a bed at the other end of the small room, and I gently threw him onto it, putting my hand up and growling, "Stay!" as soon as he landed. My cuts and scrapes were already healing, and I let a little glow into my eyes to give my words some weight. I did not want to have to subdue the human.

"What the fuck are you?" he hissed. He looked ready to launch himself at me again, despite asking what I was, not who I was.

"Just… Stay still for a minute and let me think," I murmured. Fuck. A human captive. This complicated things.

"Probably can't burn the house down now…" I mumbled to myself, sighing. "Liam is gonna be so annoyed if he has to deal with a human investigation again."

"Burn the fucking place to the ground," the man spat. "Just let me go."

I looked at him, raising my eyebrows. He was a petite and wiry little thing, but I could tell he had reached maturity, although he was probably only in his early twenties. Surely he had family and friends who were looking for him. "Don't you want the police involved? Won't your family wonder where you've been?" I asked.

He leaned back against the wall, folding his arms across his chest defensively. He was skinny, but he looked in good health otherwise, and I wondered how long he'd been held here—I didn't think it was terribly long. He was frightened, but he certainly wasn't broken. I felt a sense of satisfaction that I might have stopped whatever Marcus had planned for this human. I knew Marcus had done some terrible things to others, but perhaps this one was relatively unscathed.

Aside from the kidnapping and being held in a cellar, of course. That sort of thing was probably a bit traumatic.

"Just let me go," he said again, a frown marring his face.

"Well, that would definitely make things easier," I mused. Still, I didn't think humans found other humans being held captive and just let them go. If he ran straight to the police and described me… Well, that would be an annoyance.

I had no desire to leave Paradise Falls. Toby lived there.

"Where will you go?" I asked.

He stared at me mulishly.

"Do you have family or anyone looking for you?" I asked.

"Oh, yeah, yup, tons of people looking for me," he lied.

I tilted my head. "You aren't very good at lying."

"You aren't very good at pretending to be a normal human," he scowled.

I smiled. "I like you. You're feisty."

He rolled his eyes up, muttering, "Great, the weird guy with glowing eyes who wants to burn the house down likes me. Isn't it my lucky day."

"Oh, I don't like you like that," I answered. "I mean, I'm sure you're cute and all, but I'm actually interested in someone else." I didn't want him getting the wrong idea, after all.

He looked at me incredulously. "Are you for real?" he asked.

"If you'd like to think of me as a hallucination, this might be easier,"

I pondered. Then I discarded the thought. "Nope. Can't chance it," I sighed. "Well, you'll just have to come with me."

He stared at me, mouth slightly open. I picked up my bag and made an after-you gesture to him.

"You're totally going to kill me. Shoot me in the back of the head or something, right? Is this some kind of mob thing?" the man said, but he was getting off the bed anyway.

I frowned at him. "I would never use a gun," I answered. "What's the fun in that? Plus, I would never kill someone from behind. Humans ought to know when they're going to die. And anyway, you aren't like Marcus. I'm not going to kill you."

"Damn straight I'm not like that fucking asshole," the man muttered, and he walked out ahead of me.

"Don't run. I'm faster than you," I muttered. I didn't want to chase him down. That would be annoying. "Plus I'll find you wherever you go," I added.

"You are super fucking creepy, dude," he muttered, but he kept winding his way through the cellar.

When we reached the stairs and climbed up, I took a moment to let my flame loose in the wine cellar. I should probably go upstairs and burn the body, but I'd already burned all traces I might've left behind, so even if the fire was put out, it wasn't like any clues would lead to me. Plus, with all that alcohol, the house would go up pretty quickly.

By the time we reached the bar room, the fire was already raging. The man turned around, mumbling, "What the fuck?"

"Fire," I answered. "Follow me," I added, walking out the sliding doors. The dogs greeted me, wagging their tails. Ah, I'd forgotten about them too.

I sighed. So many complications. This was what came from not planning things out. I really knew better. But that kiss with Toby had just completely frazzled my brains.

"Alright everyone, come on. You'll all fit in the car, and I know someone who owes me a favor. He'll know what to do with you. Hopefully," I mused.

The man gave me another incredulous look, but he and the dogs both followed me off the property. We found a small gate to exit the grounds, which I burned the lock off of, and off we went into the night.

The house was a blazing inferno by the time we were walking down the street, and I heard sirens in the distance as I ushered the crew into my car.

The coffee shop owner owed me a favor after I helped him with the whole demon thing. Surely taking in a stray human and two dogs would be acceptable payment. This guy wasn't the first stray I'd rehomed, and I usually found a good soul to take care of them. I knew the coffee shop owner fit the bill there.

I decided not to call ahead, and we made the hour drive back to Paradise Falls in silence. The man pretended to fall asleep, and he might have even dozed off at one point. Both dogs were happily curled up on the back seat.

By the time we made it to the coffee shop, it looked like it was just after closing, but luckily I could see the owner inside along with his angel.

"We're here," I told everyone, climbing out and opening the car doors for the human and the dogs before walking up to the shop. I rapped against the door as the man and the dogs trailed behind me.

The coffee shop owner came over and opened the door.

"Oracle," I said, realizing I wasn't really sure of his name. If he'd told me, I'd forgotten. Come to think of it, I hadn't gotten the captive man's name either. Oops. That was probably something normal humans did.

"Hellhound," the coffee shop owner replied.

"I found this human locked in a basement, and the dogs no longer have an owner, so I thought maybe you'd like them," I said.

"You have got to be fucking kidding me," the coffee shop owner replied, looking at me, then the man, and then the dogs. He was speechless after that, and I didn't think it was the good sort of speechless.

Well, this wasn't going quite as well as I'd hoped. I waved the man and the dogs into the shop, and the owner let us through, still looking dumbfounded. He did close and lock the door behind us though.

"Alright. Tell me everything," the coffee shop owner said.

Humans—they always wanted explanations and shit. I sighed. At this rate I'd never get back to the house to see what Toby was up to.

CHAPTER 7

TOBY

I was probably a little drunk. Maybe. Buzzed at the least.

"I can't believe the serial killer kissed you," Sebbie muttered.

"Yup," I replied, popping the p dramatically. "Right at the kitchen island. Smooch. Lots of really good kissing."

"I thought we decided he was a military operative?" Josh cut in.

Sebbie just waved his hand dismissively. He might've been a little buzzed too.

Josh snorted. We were sprawled across my living room, all drinking. They had both taken a rideshare over to my house, but I don't think Josh had drunk more than a half a glass of wine.

"Refills!" I called out, standing up.

"Nah, I'm good," Josh answered.

Sebbie pouted. "Party pooper. Barely drinking, and you've been on your phone for half the night. Is someone dying or something?"

I almost spurted the wine I'd been drinking out my nose, and I choked a bit, coughing out, "Sebbie!"

Sebbie just shrugged. "What? Like I haven't noticed that I'm super bad luck," he murmured glumly.

"You are not!" I insisted. "You're our bestest friend in the whole world, and we've had all sorts of good things happen. Like Serial Killer Neighbor kissing me!"

I walked over and smacked Josh in the arm. He flinched and grabbed his arm, but I really hadn't smacked him that hard. "Sorry," I murmured.

He just smiled at me then turned to Sebbie. "You're not bad luck, Sebbie. You tried to save that guy's life. It's not your fault that he died or that the guy you were on a date with was an asshole. We've all had asshole dates. Don't let it get to you."

"I guess so," Sebbie muttered. "Still, you gotta admit, lots of people end up getting injured around me. Or dying."

"Well, maybe you're really a super powerful warlock who has the ability to save lives so the magical entity that controls the world keeps throwing injuries into your path," I said. "Ohh, or maybe you're being watched by a super secret society, and they're ascertaining your power level before they recruit you for their world-saving missions. Or—"

"And we've lost him to plotting," Josh cut in.

I ignored him and started looking around for my notebook. Or my phone. I should totally write some of these ideas down.

"Yup, we have," Sebbie laughed. "And yeah, I know there's plenty of guys out there. I'm just on a string of bad luck in the dating department. But seriously, Josh, what's up with you?"

I stopped searching around for my phone and looked at Josh. Sebbie was right—Josh had been off tonight.

It was Josh's turn to sort of shrug. "Rick and I are just having a little disagreement."

Sebbie and I looked at each other. Neither of us liked Rick. At all. The guy was just an asshole. He was loud and rude, and it seemed like he was constantly putting Josh down in the guise of joking around. We tried not to butt into each other's love lives without being asked, though. I'm sure Josh knew we weren't fond of Rick, but we tried for his sake.

"Everything ok?" I asked. "You wanna talk about it?"

"Not really," Josh admitted. "I'm sure it'll be fine. It just has me out of sorts tonight. I'm sorry if I'm a party pooper."

"Pfft," Sebbie spit out, waving his arm haphazardly. "You can always be a party pooper with us, Josh. We're your besties. If you can't poop at parties with besties, then who can you party poop with?"

I giggled at Sebbie's words, and even Josh couldn't help smiling. So maybe Sebbie had drunk a little more wine than me. No more refills; he hated being hungover.

He laughed along with us, saying, "You know what I mean."

"I do," Josh said quietly. "Thank you, guys. I should probably get going, though. Seb, you can always grab a rideshare separately if you wanna stay later."

It wasn't even that late, but Josh and Sebbie had been here for a couple hours, and if I was gonna be productive tomorrow, it probably was time to call it a night. Still, I pouted at Josh anyway.

He chuckled—he totally didn't fall for my pouting, and then I heard a car door.

"Ohmygod!" I whisper-yelled. "It's probably the neighbor! You guys can totally see my sexy neighbor!"

"Why are we whispering?" Sebbie whispered back.

Josh snorted. "You two whisper at the volume that most people talk at. And I'm not sure if we should spy on your neighbor."

Sebbie had already made his way over to the window and was peeking out the side of the curtain, though.

"Oh my god, he isn't wearing a shirt. And he is hot. Those tattoos!" Sebbie whispered.

I ran over, pushing him out of the way. "No shirt? Ohmygod! It's like Christmas came early! Lemme see!"

"You guys are ridiculous," Josh murmured, but I noticed he shut off the living room main lights, probably so we wouldn't be so obvious looking out the window into the evening. It wasn't fully dark, but it was close to it. Luckily, Sexy Neighbor's porch light was on.

"And you're an enabler," I whispered to Josh, peeking out the window.

Sexy Neighbor was indeed shirtless, with just a pair of black jeans on. He was all muscles, and he totally did have tattoos. Some kind of symbols were tattooed all over his arms in black, and it was sexy as fuck.

"My god, look at those muscles," I murmured.

"I was looking at those muscles until you elbowed me out of the way," Sebbie grumbled.

"He's mine, Seb. You can look, but don't touch," I mumbled as Sebbie pulled the curtain over further.

"You guys, he is totally going to see you," Josh said, but I noticed he was making his way over to check out Sexy Neighbor too. "Maybe we should all go and sit on the porch like normal people, and then we can say hello," Josh suggested.

"And ogle him," Sebbie added.

"Oh my god, no, definitely not. I cannot sit and make small talk on my porch when he just kissed me this afternoon! You know how bad I am at nonchalant," I hissed. "I'll try and climb him like a tree, and you guys do not need to witness that."

"I don't think I've ever seen you climb someone like a tree," Josh said thoughtfully.

"But we have seen you hook up when we've gone to clubs," Sebbie added.

Sexy Neighbor—I really needed to start calling him Dex in my head—chose that moment to look over, and with an eep we all ducked down.

"Great," Josh said. "Now if he saw us we look even more suspicious. We couldn't have just waved?"

"You ducked too!" Sebbie hissed out.

I slowly rose up and looked out, and he was thankfully turned around.

"Oh my god, that ass," I murmured.

"Oh, let me see!" Sebbie cried out, elbowing me over.

"You guys are horrible," Josh murmured, but I noticed he was totally looking out the window to scope out Dex's ass too.

Dex lifted his arms up to stretch, and my god, those back muscles. He had tattoos there as well.

Hot. As. Fuck.

"I wanna lick over every one of those tattoos," I mumbled.

"Mmmhmmm," Sebbie added.

Then Josh's phone started buzzing continuously. Sebbie and I both looked at him, but he was decidedly not looking down at his pocket where his phone was.

"It is a cute butt," Josh mumbled, but he blushed as he said it.

The vibrating sound stopped and then picked up again a second later. My guess was that his dick of a boyfriend was looking for him.

We all sort of sighed and backed away from the window.

"I probably need to go," Josh murmured.

"I'll go with you," Sebbie said. "We can share a ride back."

"That's ok. You don't have to. I'm ordering the rideshare now," Josh said, walking off with his phone out, probably to use the bathroom before he left.

I turned to Sebbie when I heard the bathroom door shut. "Try and find out what's going on," I whispered, trying to not whisper-yell.

"I will," Sebbie sighed. "I just don't… I don't want to alienate him. I don't think things are good, and I don't think pushing him will help."

"Maybe not. But I worry. Did you see the way he flinched when I smacked his arm? It wasn't that hard," I whispered.

"You think his boyfriend is messing with him?" Sebbie asked loudly.

"Shhhh!" I whispered. "And I don't know. But Rick is a dick." Then I giggled, because, yeah, I was a little buzzed and that rhyme had been too funny.

Sebbie giggled with me, then he got serious. "I'll talk to him. Let him know we're always here and we'll never judge. I think coming from both of us it would be overwhelming, but I'll mention it when we get back to town."

"Ok," I said, and we heard the door open.

"My turn!" Sebbie cried out, running into the bathroom as Josh came back into the room.

Josh rolled his eyes then looked at me. "I really am sorry."

"No worries, Josh. You know we love you. We just want to see you happy, and I'm sorry if you and Rick are fighting. We're always here if you need to chat. Or if you need to not chat and just forget about things for a while," I said.

Josh smiled. "I know. You guys gave me a great night, and it was what I needed. Next time I promise no phone out all night."

When Sebbie came out, they both walked to the front door and I went with them, flicking on my porch light, ready to walk them to their rideshare and confirm it was the right car.

"We can confirm our rideshare on our own," Josh laughed, knowing me too well. "This isn't one of your thrillers where we get kidnapped and ravaged."

"Unfortunately," Sebbie mumbled.

We all laughed as we stepped onto the porch, and then I almost choked on my own spit when I saw Sexy Neighbor leaning over the rideshare car.

He stood up, calling out, "Paula is here for Josh?"

"Yep!" Josh called out. He and Sebbie walked down the steps, and my feet carried me forward like I didn't even have a choice in the matter.

They both gave me hugs goodbye, spoke to the driver, and got into the car. I stood a little back on the driveway, and as soon as they were in, Dex came and stood next to me.

"Text me when you guys get home!" I called out as they pulled away. I saw Josh stick his hand out the window with a thumbs up.

And then it was just me and my very sexy, shirtless neighbor standing alone in my driveway in the twilight.

CHAPTER 8

DEXTER

I watched the car pull off into the night, puzzling over Toby's friends. One of his friends smelled… odd. It wasn't anything that had set my hellhound on edge, and when I'd checked, they'd both had pure souls, so I supposed I didn't need to worry. Still, I hadn't recognized the scent of one of them. It didn't seem entirely mortal.

"So…" Toby said, rocking back and forth a bit on his heels.

I looked over and noticed that he was blushing prettily in the twilight. I resisted the urge to flex for him. It had felt nice having him and his friends admire me, although Toby's admiration was all I needed. His possessiveness had also given me a thrill. I'd liked hearing him say that I was his, and it had turned me on when he'd said he wanted to lick my tattoos.

"What were you up to?" he asked, then he blushed even more darkly.

He was so cute.

"Work," I replied, wondering how far the blush would spread against his pale skin. He was so soft and beautiful and I wanted to snuggle up to him and lick him all over.

"Without a shirt?" he asked.

"It got dirty, so I took it off after I was done working," I replied. Not a lie, just not the entirety of the situation. "I can grab a shirt…" I said, motioning toward my house.

"No!" Toby insisted, then he blushed again.

So. Damn. Cute.

"I mean, no, that's fine," he chuckled nervously. "Not like I haven't seen a shirtless guy before. I mean, I write about shirtless guys all the time. I mean, not all the time, just for sex scenes. Because I write sex scenes with guys. Obviously. Because guys have sex," he blurted.

He wiped his hand across his face, and I could hear him mutter to himself, "Pull it together, Toby."

"How's the book coming?" I asked.

"Good! Great! I mean, it's ok. Coming along," he babbled, obviously still nervous. I thought about kissing him again, but I figured that would only make him more nervous. I was all for him "climbing me like a tree," but I didn't want to make Toby feel more awkward around me. The last thing I wanted was him avoiding me.

"I was thinking about that scene we talked about," I said, hoping he'd relax if we talked about his writing.

"Oh yeah?" he asked, looking at me curiously.

"Yeah, the bloodbath one? Blood on the walls and floor and all that?" I reminded him.

"Yup," he answered. "What were you thinking?"

"Well, it occurred to me that you should make sure the floor isn't carpeted. That would totally soak up some of the blood and it wouldn't pool near as well," I told him. "Also, if you're looking for blood spray, that would mainly be arteries, and your character would bleed out much quicker, so you'll probably have a lot more of the blood dripping than actually spraying," I added helpfully.

"Yeah, my character doesn't die…" he trailed off, obviously thinking.

I waited, staring at him in the moonlight. He was so beautiful. I had the urge to show him my hellhound, which was a strange desire, and my eyes must have flashed red, because he glanced over at me. I schooled my expression and made sure everything was normal, and he just sort of shook his head at himself.

"Toby, your imagination," he mumbled to himself softly. Then he looked up at me again. "Yeah, I don't think I specified what the floor was, but I'll have to check, and I think I'll make sure I show that it's concrete or something. I also liked the idea of the bad vampire smearing the blood around, so the villain does a lot of that, but I do think I have some spraying of blood. I'll have to look at the scene again."

"Sorry," I murmured, feeling bad he'd have to go back and rewrite things.

He waved a hand at me, smiling. "Are you kidding? I'd rather rewrite it than have my readers crucify me for a bad scene." He frowned a bit at that, then shook himself off.

"Let me know how it turns out," I said, seeing that he was already halfway in his head about the book.

He looked at me and smiled. "Ok, I definitely will. I'll just… I'll go work on that now," he muttered.

I had such an urge to kiss him again in the moonlight, but I only smiled instead. I was going to take things slow. I could definitely do that.

He smiled back, gave a little wave, and then turned to walk back up his porch. I watched until he was safely inside and I heard the door lock, then I turned and headed into my own home.

I stood looking out my window and watching as lights went on and off in Toby's home. It seemed he was in his living room, probably sitting and writing on his couch. I hoped his scene turned out well. If only he'd left the curtain partly open…

My thoughts were interrupted by a buzzing in my pocket. I sighed. People didn't usually call me, so this couldn't be good.

I dug out my phone and saw Liam's name on the screen. I scrubbed a hand across my face before answering.

"Took you long enough to answer," he muttered before I even had a chance to say hello. I could hear the clacking of keys in the background, and I figured he was doing his computer magic. Liam embraced technology and was our go to person.

I just preferred to burn the shit up. Much easier that way.

"What?" I responded. I wasn't in the mood for Liam. He had somewhere along the way decided he was the big brother of the pack, and it could be annoying. I loved him, but I wasn't in the mood for a million questions or a lecture.

"Are you working?" he asked.

"Nope," I answered.

"Can I guess that a small mansion going up in flames is your work?" he asked.

I made a noncommittal sound. How did he even know I was in this state, never mind near that city?

He obviously knew me well, because he answered that question before I could even ask. I'd think he could read minds, but Corbin was the one with witch blood, not Liam.

"Jude said you were in Paradise Falls, and that you described it as 'nice.' He was like a puppy in his excitement, and he spilled the details without meaning to," Liam told me.

"Of course he did," I mumbled.

"He also said you were asking about how to talk to a human," Liam added.

I made another noncommittal sound. Liam was such a nosy fucker.

Liam sighed. "Dex," he said simply.

I rolled my shoulders, letting go of my tension. Liam didn't mean any harm, and he wouldn't stop me from doing my work or pursuing Toby. And I did miss my pack.

"It feels right here, yes. There are a lot of demons and angels about, but they don't seem to bother us. I even dropped off a stray human with an oracle and an angel this evening, and they were quite helpful," I answered.

"A stray human?" Liam asked. "Dex, are you still taking in strays?"

"I don't actually take them in. I find them good homes," I defended.

"They're humans, not cats," Liam declared.

"So?" I asked, having no idea why he said that. Of course they weren't cats. Duh. Although this last human had been a snarling, hissing little thing that kind of reminded me of a cat.

"Dex, you can't just take in stray humans like they're pets. We've had this conversation," Liam reminded me.

"I don't take them in. I find them good homes. Besides, what should I have done? Left the guy locked in the wine cellar?" I asked.

"He was locked in the wine cellar?" Liam questioned.

"And I know how much you hate it when you have to go in and deal with the human databases and shit, so I found him a good home without involving the human police. It'll be fine," I reassured him.

"By all the nine hells," Liam muttered. Then I heard some clacking again. "What's his name?" he asked.

"Ummm…" I trailed off.

I thought I heard a light banging sound, and it didn't take much to guess that Liam was probably knocking his head against his desk. It was a weird human habit he'd acquired.

"You don't even know his name?" he asked, "For fuck's sake, Dex."

"What? It was busy, what with the torture and then the rescue and the dogs and the burning down of the house," I defended.

"There were dogs?" Liam asked. "Did you keep those?"

"Nah, I gave those to the oracle too," I added, hoping that would reassure him.

"Ok, what's the oracle's name then," Liam asked, and I could hear the lack of faith in his voice.

"Cassius," I said, proud to know the answer to one of his questions. The coffee shop owner had introduced himself to the other human, so I had caught his name.

"Cassius…" Liam trailed off.

"Yup. Cassius," I answered back.

"For the love of demons, Dex," Liam grunted. "Do you have a fucking last name?"

"Uh, no? I mean, how many Cassius's can there be in Paradise Falls who own a coffee shop?" I asked. He was the technology wizard. Surely it couldn't be that hard to find the answer to that.

"He owns a coffee shop?" Liam asked, fingers still typing away.

Had I not mentioned that? I was pretty sure I had mentioned that, but even if I had, when Liam was in this kind of mood, best not to rile him up.

"Yup," I just answered, and then I tucked the phone into my shoulder and wandered into the kitchen. I was guessing Toby would be up writing for a while, and I was feeling rather hungry after the night's activities. I opened the fridge and pulled out some steak. I thought I had some potatoes laying around, and that would be easy enough to throw together.

Liam was mumbling to himself, the clacking of keys still the background sound to our phone call. I started rummaging around in the pantry for the potatoes, then began the washing and cutting process. The steak wouldn't take long, and I'd probably just fry up the potatoes too.

"Got it!" Liam cried out cheerfully.

"You found him?" I asked.

"Yup!" Liam proudly announced.

"Now what?" I asked. I wasn't sure what the point of this all was.

Liam sighed. "Now I can keep an eye on him, of course. And hopefully find out some information about the other human as well."

"Why?" I asked. "Cassius is an oracle, and he's shacked up with an angel. I found the stray a nice, loving home, and I'm sure he'll be fine."

"He's not a cat, Dex," Liam reminded me. "And he's with an angel, too? I don't know about leaving a human with an afterlifer."

I knew he wasn't a cat. I didn't know why Liam felt the need to keep reminding me of that. "Obviously he isn't a cat," I answered. "And not all afterlifers are bad. I left the last stray I picked up with a couple of demons, and they're all very happy together."

"For fuck's sake, Dex," Liam mumbled, and I heard the tell-tale thumping again.

"What? I check in on them and stuff. They're lesser demons and are good souls. They wouldn't sacrifice him or anything," I added helpfully.

"I'm not sure why I'm going to bother, but do you happen to know their names?" Liam grumbled.

Shit. I mean, I had known their names. I just… wasn't very good with names. That was all. Such a pesky human detail to try and remember.

"I said that I check in with them. No need to do your computer check-ups on them," I grumbled.

Liam muttered some more before he asked me for my address. I begrudgingly gave it to him.

"Hmmm, looks like only two houses nearby. You think either owner would sell? The area is backed up to protected forest land, so we wouldn't have to worry about developments. It's large property areas too. This could definitely work…" he trailed off, keys clicking away.

I was chopping potatoes and grabbing spices and answered without thinking. "I think the old lady might sell, but I don't want Toby moving."

"Toby?" Liam asked.

Shit.

"Yes, he's the one neighbor," I said, hoping Liam would leave it there.

"Would he happen to be the one you were asking Jude how to talk to?" Liam questioned.

"Hmmm," I replied noncommittally. "Well, I gotta run. I'm starved, and steak is calling my name. I'll be in touch if I need you."

Liam did some grumbling, then muttered about looking into buying at least one of the houses, and then he thankfully got off the phone without any more questions. I would guess he would also be doing a background check on Toby, but I wasn't worried about that. I didn't even know why he bothered when we could see someone's soul, but Liam liked doing background checks—it made him feel human. Eh, to each their own.

I threw the steak and thinly sliced potatoes on, thinking back to Toby. I wondered if there were any other details he needed for his book? I'd have to find my way outside next time he ordered a delivery so I could run into him and check.

Stalkerish? Maybe. But I didn't think Toby would mind running into me again. And I was always happy to be helpful with research for his books.

A hellhound's job was never done.

CHAPTER 9

TOBY

I finished revising my scene and tried not to think about Dex without a shirt.

All those muscles. And the tattoos. And he smelled really good. And he was super helpful when it came to my work.

There weren't honestly that many people I could talk to about my writing. Josh and Sebbie were proud of me and respected all that I'd accomplished, but they were more amused by my random ramblings. They didn't actually help me. They joked about me following the trails of plot bunnies and laughed at my macabre search history, but it just wasn't their thing. And that was totally fine. When Josh started talking about spreadsheets, my eyes glazed over in boredom, but I still listened.

That's what friends did.

Still, it was really cool to have someone who was so interested and helpful. Of course, Amy, my PA was super helpful too, but she had a ton of clients, and I hated to bother her with random stuff unless I was really stuck. She handled all my social media and my releases, and she was a godsend for doing it.

Who knew that being an author was so much more than writing books?

Still, I couldn't complain. I was doing what I loved, and I made a successful living at it.

That reminded me that I probably needed to let Amy know about the most recent email. She had been the one to actually block him on my socials, since she had the sign in for all those accounts and monitored them more closely than me, especially when I was in the middle of writing a book. I should probably forward the email to her as well.

I opened my inbox to do just that, and I saw that there were more messages.

As in, numerous messages.

I opened the first one and skimmed it, then went through the rest. I felt sicker as I read each one, snippets of them jumping out at me and blazing across my mind.

I'm your biggest fan.

I'm sure that bitch of a PA is the one who blocked me. I know you would never do that to me. Hopefully she isn't checking your email, too. Don't worry, I'll find some way around that bitch.

I'm sure it's lonely being an author, but I'll keep you company and provide inspiration for ALL your scenes.

I can protect you and take care of you just like Carlos did for Antoine in your book.

Because that was the stalker guy from my book that he'd already referenced. I felt like screaming. That was fiction. This was real life. Stalking was not sexy. Ok, so maybe being a bit stalkerish about my neighbor was sexy, but hey, we knew each other, so that didn't count as stalking. I almost giggled hysterically, and I knew I had to pull it together.

I counted the emails. Ten. He'd sent me ten emails in the span of twenty-four hours.

What. The. Fuck.

What was I supposed to do with this? What could I do with this?

I had no idea what the guy's name was or where he was from, and it was only a small consolation that he had no idea what my real name was either.

I forwarded the emails to Amy and started pacing. I ended up walking around and checking to make sure all my windows and doors were locked before heading up to my bedroom. I locked myself inside and sat on my bed, staring at the door.

I was being absurd, because he didn't know who I was. There was no way for him to know who I was.

Fuck. Had I actually acquired a stalker?

I wrote dark romance and suspense. I was popular in my genres, but I wasn't getting interviewed on tv or anything. I was no Stephen King, for fuck's sake. I wasn't supposed to get a stalker. I was plain, and boring, and I ate too many potato chips and lived like a hermit. I barely even made it onto social media, letting Amy take care of most of that.

As if on cue, my phone rang.

I might've jumped a bit, and then giggled a little hysterically. I answered my phone.

"Toby." Amy's voice sounded like she was scolding me, and I put my head in my hands.

"I know," I murmured.

"Toby, this is serious," she pronounced.

"I know!" I stated. "I haven't heard anything for ages!"

"Well…" Amy sort of trailed off.

Great. What the fuck didn't I know?

"Amy," I grumbled, "you blocked him on all my socials."

"I did," she stated firmly. "And when he made a new account and joined and sent you a private message, I blocked that account too."

"Are you serious? You didn't tell me?" I asked.

Amy sighed. "Toby, I knew you'd just worry. And it was a lot of hateful shit that you did not need to read. I replied and told him that your PA handled all social media and he would be blocked. I kind of figured he was just irate that you blocked him, and I thought if he could blame someone else he would lay off and wouldn't blast you in reviews or anything. I know you specifically said you were worried about that. I was trying to help!"

"Did you save the message?" I asked.

Maybe we could take the emails and the social media messages to the cops, although really, I'd done enough research over time to know there wasn't much they could do. They weren't going to devote a detective to a few creepy emails, and everyone had their servers blocked or encrypted or whatever the fuck it was called these days, so chances of learning who the guy was from the emails were extremely slim.

Gotta love technology.

Fuck.

"I should have saved them," Amy replied. "Honestly, I just wanted it gone before you saw it, because I knew you'd panic, and you were in the middle of edits at the time. I was trying to help!"

"Fuck," I muttered, getting up and pacing. "I know. That was it, though? Just the one message that you replied to?"

"Well…" Amy hesitated.

"Amy!" I hissed. "I am freaking the fuck out here!"

"I know. Just… take a deep breath. Stay calm. You don't use your real name on the internet, and the guy is just sending creepy emails. I'll call your local police station and forward everything to them, and I'll tell them about the social media stuff and the message I deleted. I don't know how far we'll get…"

"Not far," I muttered, "but at least we'll have documented it."

"I think… I think he's probably tried to rejoin a few times since then with fake accounts," Amy said carefully.

"Amy!" I hissed again.

"I can't be sure! I make it a policy to not let anyone who has just created an account into your groups or socials, because they end up being spammers. After I blocked him, for a few days there were a lot of requests from new accounts, but I can't be sure. Anyway, he gave up, so I figured he moved on," Amy defended.

"I'm freaking out," I said, continuing to pace back and forth.

"Listen Toby, relax. The guy doesn't know who you are. It's a creepy internet fan, but I'll call the local police in the morning and file a report. I have more information than you, so it makes sense. I'll keep you posted, ok? Just breathe and try not to panic," she said.

I blew a breath out. That was easier said than done. Amy tried to calm me down by talking about my current project and the logistics of my next release. I let myself get distracted by those details, and we talked about a new series I was thinking about.

By the time we got off the phone, I was feeling calmer and had stopped pacing. I was about to get undressed for the shower when I remembered my PO box.

I'd emptied it just the other day when I went into town, and of course I'd been too lazy to bother going through the mail at the time.

It was sitting downstairs in a tote bag. I hadn't even rifled through the envelopes yet. I knew I had a few copyrights due in from the Copyright Office, and I often exchanged stickers of my characters and fun stuff like that with other authors, and I received some junk mail, so I hadn't really put it at the top of my list.

But what if my stalker fan had sent something?

I had a PO Box for all author related stuff, and I didn't think it would be impossible for someone to track it down. That's why I'd used a PO Box and not my home address.

It was going to bother me now until I went and checked. The blue reusable tote bag was taking on sinister proportions in my head.

What if he sent a bomb?

No, I didn't have any packages, only envelopes. So no bomb. But wasn't there a thing on the news ages ago where people were sent anthrax or something? Maybe he sent me anthrax or some other poison. I'd open an envelope and powder would float out and I'd be dead.

Although he didn't seem to want to just kill me—he seemed to want to stalk me and probably kidnap me before eventually killing me. So maybe there'd be some sort of sleeping powder in the envelope.

Or maybe I was being delusional and letting my imagination run away with me. Again. Perils of being an author, I supposed.

I took a deep breath and headed downstairs. I'd have to check or I'd just work myself into an anxiety spiral of doom over it.

I grabbed the bag from by the door where I'd left it and walked it into the living room, dumping it out onto the coffee table. It was pretty easy to spot the junk mail, and I got rid of that. That left me with about seven envelopes.

Three of them had return addresses of other authors I recognized. Down to four mystery letters.

The first one was a bunch of character stickers and a bookmark. I almost rolled my eyes at Jay for not putting his return address on the envelope. The character stickers were super cute though, but I put them aside.

Second envelope was junk mail disguised as something interesting. Stupid junk mail.

Third envelope was fan mail. I opened it and skimmed it, then went back and read it more slowly. It was a very complimentary letter, but of course the person requested some swag. They even had a folded up self-addressed envelope inside, so I set that aside. It certainly wouldn't hurt to send them a few stickers.

One envelope left. It took on epic proportions of dread in my mind. It was always the last envelope in my books, but what were the odds it was from Creepy Guy in real life? Because this was real life, not one of my novels or a horror movie. The power wasn't going to go off, there wasn't a serial killer out on the loose (well, unless you counted my very hot neighbor, but jury was still out on whether he was a serial killer), and there wasn't someone hiding in my attic.

Fuck. Now I was gonna totally worry about the damn attic. Why did I do this to myself?

I sighed and picked up the last envelope. I opened it carefully, and of course no white powder floated out.

There were only two sentences written inside, and it was handwritten in a pretty cursive on a plain piece of paper. My heart raced at the sight of it, and I noticed my hands were shaking a bit.

I placed the sheet of paper down and looked at the envelope. It was postmarked from a city not even an hour away.

It was ok. I'd tell Amy, and I'd bring this to the police station if I needed to, not that I thought there was much they were gonna be able to do. I took some deep breaths, walked to the pantry, grabbed a bag of chips, and headed upstairs. I'd shower and then get comfy clothes on and snack in bed (fuck the crumbs for once) and find the best, most graphic romance I could lay my hands on to lose myself in.

My plan almost worked, but even though the book I chose was really good with great sex scenes, the lines from the letter just kept looping in my head.

Don't worry Toby, I'm sure we'll be seeing each other soon. We were meant to be together.

CHAPTER 10

Something was wrong with Toby.

I hadn't seen my cute neighbor for the past two days, ever since he'd sent his friends off into the night. I might've worried that he was avoiding me, only it wasn't just that he wasn't going out.

I don't think Toby had left his bedroom much in the past two days. He didn't have any food delivered, which was extremely odd for him. I hadn't heard his phone ring, which meant he either put it on silent or he wasn't taking calls. I hadn't heard any phone conversations, and usually he didn't go more than half a day without calling someone. Granted, it was hard for me to hear conversations clearly when he was in his bedroom, but usually I could still make out the muffled sound of voices.

I could see lights turning on and off, and I didn't smell the rot of decay, so I knew he wasn't seriously injured or dead.

Still, something wasn't right. My hellhound was… agitated. I felt protective of Toby, and I knew I walked around half of the day with my eyes glowing red. My hellhound was an itch underneath my skin, demanding to come out.

No one needed my hellhound form going to check on Toby.

I finally gave in; I could go knock on his door, but I wasn't sure I had a good excuse. Didn't people need an excuse to do that? Did people really go borrow a cup of sugar? Maybe I could ask if he had some coffee I could borrow? Surely that was a reasonable thing to do.

I just needed to keep my hellhound under wraps so I didn't scare the pretty human.

What if Toby was hurt? Or sick? Humans got sick. Sometimes they even died from sickness, even if they were young.

I growled low in my throat. Toby sick or hurt was not an option. I slipped my boots on near the door and headed over to his place, knocking loudly on the door when I got there.

I waited. I heard footsteps from the bedroom upstairs heading toward the window, light and tentative, only he wouldn't see me with the porch overhang. I jumped off the porch and looked up to the window, only he was no longer there.

I climbed the porch steps and knocked again, leaning in to look through the door.

That's when I smelled it—fear.

I growled, and I knew my eyes were red. Toby was afraid, and the urgency to go to him was pounding in my body.

I tried the door handle, which was locked. It took only a little bit of my strength to force it open, cracking the door jam. I would worry about that later.

"Toby!" I cried as I ran into his house.

I heard a whimper of distress, and I was halfway up the stairs to check on him when he appeared at the top of the stairs, pale, shaking the tiniest bit, reeking of fear, and wielding a butcher knife in his hand.

"Toby! Are you ok?" I asked, stopping on the steps and looking up at him.

He saw me and breathed out, his hand with the knife dropping down. In the next breath it seemed like his legs gave out and he sat down hard on the top stair, his head in his hands, the knife precariously close to his face.

"Fuck, you scared me," he breathed out.

I had been the one to scare Toby? Shit.

I was torn between going to him and backing away since I had frightened him. But he wasn't afraid of me the other day, so what had frightened him now about me? And if he was really frightened, would he have dropped down into such a vulnerable position? He wasn't even looking at me in alarm. Was it me, or was it someone knocking on his door? Was he expecting someone else?

I growled without meaning to at the thought of someone scaring Toby, and he looked up at me. Only he didn't look frightened, even with the growl. He looked… relieved.

He didn't smell scared anymore either. Since my instinct was to go comfort Toby, I slowly inched my way up the stairs. He was looking at me, and I wondered if my eyes were red. I blinked, trying to force my hellhound down, and made my way up the rest of the stairs.

Toby only stared up at me, and I slowly reached down, taking the butcher knife from his hand. He let it drop into mine without a fight, and I sat next to him on the top step. Our knees brushed against each other. I wanted to grumble in delight at the contact, only the smell of fear was still a faint odor in the air and Toby looked exhausted. He had circles under his eyes and didn't look well.

"I'm sorry if I scared you," I said carefully. "I was worried about you."

He seemed to shake off more of his nerves, and he tilted his head quizzically at me. "Worried? About me? Why?" he asked.

"I usually see you outside, and you haven't gotten take-out in two days," I answered. I couldn't very well tell him I hadn't heard him take any calls and that he hadn't left his room much.

He giggled at that, even if it did sound slightly hysterical. "Oh my god, that's so true. At least I know if I go missing my next door neighbor and food delivery will notice," he said.

"I would notice if you were gone," I said seriously, placing my hand that didn't have the butcher knife in it on his knee.

"At least someone would," he muttered. I didn't know what had Toby so spooked, but I was determined to find out. I stood up, reaching my empty hand down to Toby to help him up.

"Why don't we go grab you a glass of water or something. You can explain what's going on," I said.

He took my hand without hesitation, and my hellhound preened at the trust he put in me. I led him downstairs and let him take the lead as we walked toward the kitchen. He looked behind him, as if to make sure I was still there. When we got to the kitchen, I set the butcher knife on the island and stood leaning on it while Toby grabbed two cups and filled them with water, handing one to me. He sat down on one of the stools, and I heard him breathe out a sigh.

"I'm sorry if I scared you," I said again. I wasn't sure how to get him to share what had been going on, and I didn't want to frighten him.

"It's ok," he mumbled, his head still down. He looked up then. "I just thought you were someone else, and it made me nervous."

He had been afraid of someone else. Who was Toby scared of? He tilted his head and I realized that I was growling almost subvocally. I cut it off and slowly blinked, making sure my eyes weren't red. I was going to take care of Toby, but I needed to get my hellhound under control. I didn't need him screaming and running from fear because I was being not-human.

"Who did you think I was?" I asked, my voice gravelly and low. "Is someone bothering you?"

"Oh man, you are totally MC material," he muttered under his breath. I had no idea what "MC" was referring to, although I felt like I'd heard him use the term before when talking about his books.

"Toby, is someone threatening you?" I asked again.

Toby sighed and put his head down again. "Maybe I'm overreacting," he mumbled. "It was just a couple of emails, and the one letter to my PO box, which anyone could look up because the stupid law requires an address on newsletters, but I just got in my head and sort of spiraled about it. I'm sure it's nothing, and I really don't think the guy even knows where I live, so I'm totally overreacting," he said again.

I wasn't sure if he was trying to reassure himself or me.

"What emails?" I asked.

"Plus, the police said this thing happens all the time on the internet, and there's really nothing they can do about it. They'll file a report anyway so it's on record, but they said although the emails are threatening in nature, there is no actual stated threat or anything illegal in them." Toby giggled a little hysterically then. "Maybe if the guy had sent me a dick pic I could've complained about porn or something. Not that I want to see that," he added, "but it's just frustrating. But I knew there wasn't going to be anything they could do."

He'd filed a police report? Someone was sending him threatening emails? I growled again, and Toby tilted his head.

"And now I'm totally seeing things because I'm sleep deprived and anxious and I'm probably going slightly insane," he mumbled to himself.

I closed my eyes and gripped his kitchen island with my hands, forcing myself to remain calm. My hellhound was a pressure beneath my skin, burning to come out. I hadn't taken my other form in far too long.

Soon. But not now. Must not scare the pretty human, I thought to myself.

I took a deep breath, flexing then loosening my hands on the counter. When I was sure I had myself under control, I opened my eyes and looked at Toby, who was looking at me with a fascinated stare.

At least he didn't look scared.

"I don't like that you've been threatened. Tell me what happened," I ordered.

Ok, so maybe I wasn't completely calm, but my order didn't seem to scare Toby. If anything, I thought I saw a small smile on his face.

Then he told me all about the guy who had been stalking him. Toby didn't use the word, but that's what it was. Social media harassment, then threatening emails, and then an actual letter? The guy was escalating. I was thankful that Toby kept his real name and address private, but there were ways around that.

The guy could have followed him home from the post office, for fuck's sake, keeping a look out on the PO box in order to find out Toby's real address.

I mean, that's what I would have done if I was hunting Toby.

Which I wasn't. Of course. Because I didn't have to. He lived right next door.

He could have put a tracker on the letter as well, although I figured Toby would have noticed that. Still…

"Let me see the letter," I ground out.

He obediently got up and went into his pantry, bringing me a freezer ziplock bag with a letter and an envelope in it. He blushed adorably when I raised my eyebrows at the baggie.

"They bag it on television," he murmured. "But when Amy, my personal assistant, talked to the police, they only wanted a picture of it for evidence. I didn't even have to go down to the station." He shrugged then, handing it over.

"Send me the emails, too," I demanded.

If the police wouldn't do anything about it, then I would. It might take getting Liam involved, but that was a price I would pay. I figured someone from the pack would probably descend on me soon anyway.

Toby got up, walked into the living room to grab his computer, and came back to the kitchen, dutifully opening it up. "Where should I send them?" he asked.

I spelled out my email address for him and he began the process of forwarding the emails.

I thought about what else I could do to protect Toby. Cameras would be good. I wasn't sure I'd be able to sneak any into his house, and it was probably a little forward to ask to watch him on camera, but I could certainly place them outside. Motion sensors too. With my hearing, I probably didn't need cameras in the house anyway—I heard most things unless we were on opposite sides of our houses and he was talking quietly.

So maybe a camera somewhere in his bedroom would be a good idea. Or maybe I should just start staying over. Although I thought humans had rules about things like that. It was rather frustrating.

I would not allow the dream vision I'd had the other day to become a reality. Toby would not be kidnapped by some psycho stalker. I was the only psycho stalker he needed in his life.

I realized that was a bit unhinged, but oh well. He had the protection of a hellhound, whether he wanted it or not.

CHAPTER 11

TOBY

I continued forwarding the emails to Dex, more than a little giddy that he seemed to be taking control of the situation. Was it a little bit romance novel damsel in distress? Yes, it totally was, and I didn't give a damn. If Sexy Neighbor was going to take charge, I would happily be a damsel in distress. Except for the damsel part, obviously. Dude in distress? Gentleman in jeopardy? Mister in misery?

Whatever. The point was I felt about a thousand times better with Dex here. I'd been in a spiral of panic, feeling totally hopeless. I knew the police couldn't do much, and I knew everything was probably fine, but my anxiety had gotten the best of me, and I'd felt isolated and alone and scared.

Then Dex showed up, all knight in shining armor. Or serial killer in black clothes. The point was that he made me feel safe. I knew I was overtired and stressed and probably imagining him being all growly and eye-glowy too, but he totally reminded me of a bad-ass MC who would save the day.

Yes, I knew life wasn't a romance novel. I mean, mostly it wasn't. Romance stories really did happen in real life. Art imitated life and all that.

I finished sending the last email, determinedly not rereading them as I forwarded them. I looked up, and Dex seemed deep in thought. Should I offer him something? Thank him for his help? Beg him to ravage me over the kitchen island? Where did we go from here?

I had no fucking clue. Despite being a writer, I was really pretty bad at peopling. I gave a sigh, and that seemed to shake Dex out of his thoughts.

"I'll do my best to take care of this for you, Toby. Try not to worry," he said, stalking over towards me.

I was sitting on the kitchen island stool, and he looked down at me and was so damn close. And hot. Fuck.

It was like he sensed my thoughts, because he gave a little smirk, and then he was leaning down, and I was closing my eyes and leaning up, and thank fuck his lips pressed against mine.

My hands found their way to his chest, and he was fucking hot. Like, actually hot. The man was a furnace, but I barely had time to think about that before his arms wrapped around me and his tongue lightly traced my lips. I opened up, and his tongue gently pressed against mine.

I hated when guys just shoved it in there. Like full tongue sliding down your throat and just hanging out there, and what the hell were you supposed to do with that? Suck on it? Like was kissing only a prelude to a blow job for guys like that? Who needed a dead fish of a tongue flopping around in their mouth? It was awkward as fuck.

Dex did not kiss like that. His tongue gently teased at mine until I was pressing closer and grabbing onto his shirt. Our tongues were flirting, his lips were soft, and it was just fucking fun kissing him. He pressed forward into the kiss then eased back at intervals. Half the time I felt like chasing him, and half the time I felt like he was about to devour me.

It was hot as hell. In every sense of the word. My dick perked up, ready to get involved in the action, and when he pressed closer to me, I spread my legs without thought. The stool put his sexy as fuck abs level with my dick, and I couldn't help the groan that escaped me as he pressed against me.

I felt his mouth smile against mine, and he kissed my neck, gently nibbling at it, and I could only groan and press into him. Fuck, this man fried every fucking sense I had. I shamelessly rubbed against his abs, and his hard dick pressed against my hip, so I moved my leg up and down to rub his dick. He groaned into my neck, giving a sharp little bite that made me gasp.

I thought I might come in my pants, which was embarrassing but also so fucking hot.

I wanted this man naked and in my bed. Holy fuck, did I.

"Dex," I moaned out, and he gentled his nipping, easing back slightly.

I mewled in disappointment. I couldn't help it. I wanted him pressed up against me again, his heat searing me.

He leaned his forehead against mine, his eyes closed, and we both took a minute to catch our breaths.

He finally opened his eyes and pulled back. "I won't take advantage of you when you're scared and upset, but we aren't done, ok?" he asked.

I nodded. I really wanted him to take advantage of me—like please, please take all the advantage that he wanted. But fuck if it wasn't cute that he also wanted me to be sure and not all emotional and shit.

"Ok. If you promise," I mumbled, and I knew I sounded petulant, but I didn't care.

He chuckled, pecking me on the lips. "Oh, I promise. I want to get things started in taking care of this issue, though. I don't want you in danger, Toby."

"Me either," I mumbled as he backed away. I slid off the stool, knowing he was about to make his exit.

"I want you to call for me if you need anything, ok, Toby? Even if you're just scared and want company. Understand?" he asked.

"I don't have your number," I muttered.

He smiled, taking my phone off the counter where I'd left it and typing into it. "There. Now you do. But if you're in a bind and can't get to your phone, yell for me. Our houses aren't that far apart, and I'll hear you."

I kind of doubted it, but I nodded anyway. I followed him out to the front porch. It was warm, but I still put my arms around myself when we got outside. I just felt… unsafe.

He seemed to know it, because he looked around, seemed to sniff the air, which I knew was weird, but I swear it looked like that.

"You're safe here. No one is around our houses or has been here. Town is safe, too, at least today, but I don't want you leaving town unless you talk to me," he demanded.

"Ok," I said, not even questioning how he knew that. Did he have surveillance or something? Probably, since he was a badass military dude. Or serial killer. Or whatever.

And yeah, I was giving off total damsel in distress vibes, and I should probably put my foot down about autonomy and all that shit, but I didn't care. It felt good to have someone care.

"Maybe I'll run into town to get some groceries. Do you think that would be ok?" I asked. And to check my PO box again, because I wouldn't be able to help it. Maybe to make an appearance in the police station too, because it never hurt to let them know I was an actual person and not just a name on a case.

"Yes, that's good. Do you want me to come with you?" Dex asked.

So fucking sweet. I contemplated it for a minute, but I would rather him do whatever mojo he was gonna do with the emails and stuff. "I'll be ok, and I know most people in town. I'll be careful," I promised.

He walked over, gently held my face in his hands, and kissed me. It was soft and romantic and so fucking sweet I almost cried.

He pulled away, smiled, and vaulted off the porch, looking totally hot and badass while he did it.

"Let me know when you're back," he insisted again.

I nodded and gave a stupid little wave before turning to go back into my house. Ok, so I had a stalker. That sucked. But I also had Sexy Neighbor looking out for me and kissing me. So that was a plus.

I grabbed my wallet and keys off the side table by my front door. If I didn't go out now, I'd just get lost in either panic or in writing a great sex scene based on my kiss with Dex. Toss up as to which one would win (my brain was a weird place). But I really did need to pick up some groceries, and it would be nice to get out for a bit.

As I left, I noticed my door jam was cracked a bit, and I thought maybe that was due to Dex charging in to check on me (which I wasn't complaining about—I found it sweet that he was worried). I guess my lock wasn't very sturdy, but luckily my deadbolt still worked and it seemed mostly secure. Still, I made a mental note to fix the door (or maybe hire someone to fix it) and get better security as I got into my car.

Paradise Falls had a cute little downtown, and I generally loved living there. I wasn't gonna let some asshole stalker ruin my vibe, either. I decided to stop in the coffee shop first before hitting the little market. There was a bigger superstore market in the next town over, but I didn't need much, and I wasn't leaving town. I'd promised Dex. My neighbor who'd kissed me. Twice.

At what point did we go from flirting and kissing to more? Should I invite him over for dinner or something? That was probably the next step. Like, a date or whatever.

My thoughts were interrupted by the cute guy behind the counter. He was totally unfamiliar to me, and he also looked like he was going to glare any customers into submission. Despite his frown, he was still cute. Not nearly as hot as Dex, of course, but still cute. Cassius came bustling out of the kitchen at that moment, and he smiled and waved when he saw me.

"Toby! Haven't seen you in ages! Lost in your books?" he asked, already starting to get my favorite coffee.

The surly guy stepped back, but he kept glaring. I gave an awkward little wave. Did he know me or something? Was he not a fan?

"Don't mind Q," Cassius said, giving the man a light shove on the arm. "He's still acclimating to… everything."

The guy—Q? I swore that's what Cassius said—stopped glaring quite so much. He looked almost like he tried to smile, but I wasn't sure it was gonna work. He looked pissed off at the world. He probably had some tragic backstory. Maybe he had escaped from a religious cult that kicked out men once they reached maturity. Or maybe he was secretly on the run from evil vampires who were obsessed with the taste of his blood.

Ohhh, or maybe he was The Chosen One, and he was pissed off that he got stuck with the job, and his harem of sexy men hadn't shown up yet to help him overcome the tragic history he surely had. (Bullying, abuse, or maybe everyone he ever loved died? Something like that, I was sure.)

"He's new in town and doesn't know anyone yet," Cassius went on. He turned to the guy then. "Toby here is our resident gay author. He's good people."

The guy seemed to loosen up slightly when Cassius mentioned I was gay. Huh. Maybe he'd been raised in an overly religious household that had sent him to some horrible conversion camp and he was afraid of homophobic people.

Cassius cleared his throat. "Toby, he is not one of your characters."

I blushed, and the guy looked over at Cassius, eyebrow raising. "What does he write?" Q asked.

"Dark fantasy and paranormal romance," Cassius stated, putting my cup on the counter.

"I could totally be one of his characters," the guy mumbled, starting to ring up the coffee.

Cassius handed me a cookie, because I always got one, and our hands brushed. He grabbed onto mine, his eyes staring off into the distance for a moment. He looked at me sharply then and sniffed the air.

Q looked just as confused as I was.

"Uh," I mumbled, because this was weird. Not even like in my head making up stories weird. Just plain old weird.

Cassius let go of my hand and leaned back. "You and Dex, huh," he said, not even making it a question.

Well, wasn't that cryptic as hell. Had I told him about my neighbor? Had Josh or Sebbie? He wasn't a close friend, but we were all friendly with him. Or did I smell like Dex or something? What the hell?

"Uh, yeah?" I said, although I didn't sound too sure.

"Well, stick with him and you'll be fine," Cassius said. Q and I both stared at him. He looked at Q and said, "You know Dex."

"I do?" the man asked.

"Yes. He came in the other night."

Q looked confused, and Cassius added, "You know, the same night you came in?" The words seemed to have some kind of weight to them, because the guy flinched.

Then he looked at me, sort of squinted, and he said, "You must be the guy he likes."

"Wait, he said he likes me?" I asked, suddenly feeling giddy.

Q really did smirk then. "He is one creepy fucking dude," he said, but it was more respectful than mean.

I smiled at him. "Yeah. It's so hot, isn't it?" I asked.

Q chuckled then, and Cassius looked at both of us and just sighed. "Off with you, Toby. Coffee and cookie are on the house. Just stick with Dex, and life will be just fine," he said, then he started whistling and headed over to wipe down the counter.

Q and I gave each other a look—Cassius was weird, but I was kind of used to it. Apparently Q was too. With that, I took my cookie and headed off to the supermarket.

Hopefully that trip would be less eventful than getting coffee was. I needed chips, and probably some real food too, but I was ready to head back home. Maybe I'd ask Dex to come over for dinner once I actually had groceries in the house. Surely I could manage to cook something without burning it.

Chapter 12

As soon as I walked in the door, I grabbed my computer and headed out onto my front porch. I sat on the porch swing and started doing some online research, eventually ordering some top of the line security, rush shipping so that it would be here tomorrow for me to install. If I obsessively sniffed the air, well… I was just being cautious.

I could smell a rotting soul miles away, and I'd felt confident at the time telling Toby he could go into town. It wasn't that far, and I hadn't sensed anything. But now doubts were starting to creep in. What if the stalker wasn't fully rotting yet? I hadn't sensed any decaying souls either, which was actually really rare for a town and one of the reasons Paradise Falls was so welcoming. Usually there were souls who were decaying and could go either way in most towns, but Paradise Falls seemed to genuinely be a good place. I didn't know if all the demons and angels and the oracle somehow scared off bad souls, but the town smelled nice.

Nevertheless, if the guy had never actually done anything, and if his intentions toward Toby hadn't turned malicious, then maybe he wouldn't smell like decay. People had weird and terrible thoughts all the time, and some online bullying and trolling wasn't enough to make a soul decay. If that had been the case, I thought the human race would've been doomed. But everyone made mistakes, and most humans were redeemable. We only went after the ones who were beyond that point.

At any rate, I still didn't smell decay, and with how creepy and malicious the stalker seemed, I thought his ill intentions would have affected his soul.

Maybe I should put a tracker on Toby. Just a little one. Surely that was ok, wasn't it?

I started searching the internet, but it wasn't long before I realized my next step was going to be dealing with Liam. Not only did he know tech equipment better, but I also needed to get him in on the emails.

I sighed and picked up my phone, but before I could even dial, it rang. I looked at it stupidly for a moment before hitting the green button and grunting into the phone.

"Well hello to you too," I heard.

"Oracle," I said hesitantly. "There are no returns allowed."

He snorted into the phone. "First of all, I have a name, as I told you the other night. Second of all, I'm not returning Q."

"What's a Q?" I asked.

"Give me strength to deal with idiotic hellhounds," he muttered to himself.

I growled into the phone at him, but I don't think it did much good.

"Q is the guy you dropped off on my porch, hellhound. And he's settling in just fine. Sort of. I'm sure you were super concerned and all," he grumped.

"I knew you'd take care of him. You're a good soul. I never leave strays with humans who won't take care of them," I defended.

"Strays?" he sputtered. "He isn't a freaking dog, Dexter."

Ah, so he remembered my name. That was nice.

"Yes, Cassius," I replied, emphasizing his name, because I wanted to show him I wasn't clueless. "I'm well aware he isn't a dog. Or a cat. And I don't know why people keep talking about stray humans like that. It's pretty disrespectful, you know."

Cassius sputtered and mumbled to himself some more, and I continued looking up tiny tracking devices I might be able to slip on Toby. Maybe one on his car and one in his wallet? And on his cell phone. It would be even better if it was on him, since a kidnapper would surely take everything away. I wondered if I could get him microchipped. Huh—that would actually solve everything. I pondered it for a moment.

Nah, that was probably a bit much. He'd probably notice if he fell asleep suddenly and woke up with a small scar. I shrugged to myself and was about to continue my search, but Cassius apparently got his shit together enough to get to the point.

"Toby was here," he finally said.

I perked up at that. "Was he ok?" I asked, and I knew my voice was more guttural. I really needed a run in my hellhound form after this.

"He was fine," Cassius reassured me. "I take it you know that he's in some sort of danger?"

"Yes," I ground out. "Did you get anything specific?"

"No, unfortunately. Just a sense of danger and then a whiff of smoke with a feeling of safety. When I came back to myself, I realized he actually did smell like you, so I figured you were already on your way to marking him," Cassius responded.

"Marking him?" I asked. Could I mark him? Was there something I didn't know?

"Oh, look at that, time to go! Q is fine, the dogs are fine, and I'm sure you'll keep Toby safe! Bye!" Cassius rushed out, hanging up before I could ask any more questions.

Fucking oracles and seers. So damn annoying. They never told you what you needed to know.

I knew I needed to call Liam, but I was kind of obsessively sniffing the air now, and I was debating getting in my car and heading into town to find Toby when I heard his car in the distance. I closed my laptop and sat nonchalantly on my porch.

When Toby drove up, I could see the relief on his face when he saw me on the porch. That was good, at least.

He got out of the car, and I jumped off the porch, strutting a bit when I smelled Toby's arousal. He was so fucking cute.

He blushed prettily and then opened his back door, grabbing a bag. I walked over and grabbed the rest out of his car. He just sort of stared at me, and I made the go ahead motion with my head. I didn't have his key after all. Not yet, anyway.

"Oh, yeah, duh, sorry," he mumbled, rushing up the porch and opening the door. I noticed the slight crack in the doorframe where I'd broken it and reminded myself to fix that as I went in and put the bags down on his table.

"Everything ok in town?" I asked.

"Yeah…" he said, starting to unpack the groceries and shoving stuff into the fridge. I sensed his hesitation.

"What is it? Did someone bother you?" I growled.

Toby chuckled nervously. "No, no, nothing like that. There wasn't even anything in my PO box."

I growled again. "Don't check it again without me," I ordered. That was a way to find Toby, and I didn't trust it.

He stared at me, and I slow blinked, making sure my eyes were normal. Fuck. I was totally losing control. I felt like a fucking puppy around Toby, but I couldn't help it.

"Ok," he breathed out, still staring.

"What spooked you?" I asked.

He chuckled nervously then, starting to unload the groceries again. "It's probably nothing. It's just that Mrs. Dillinger told me that Edna told her that Patricia got an offer on her house this morning."

I had no fucking clue what he was talking about. Was I supposed to know these humans?

I grunted in response.

"And I'm sure it's not a big deal," Toby went on. "Patricia has been wanting to move south to be closer to her grandkids for a while—she's always talked about it. It's just that I didn't know she'd even listed the house. I mean, I didn't see a for sale sign or anything."

I grunted again. Did Toby want to buy the house? Was that why he was concerned? Did he want to move away from me? I growled a little at the thought, and Toby looked at me.

"So you think it's concerning?" he asked, closing the fridge and staring at me across the kitchen.

"You want to move into Patricia's house?" I questioned, trying to maintain my composure.

"Why would I want to do that?" he asked, looking confused. "I mean, her house is nice, and it's a little more private than mine, being further back in the woods, but I like my house. I can't imagine moving all my stuff just to be your neighbor on the other side." Toby went over to the bags and grabbed some stuff for the pantry, adding, "And her house isn't as close to yours as mine is. Not that it matters or anything, because obviously I wouldn't choose a house based on how close it was to yours. Because that would be, like, stalkerish or something," he laughed, hiding his head in the pantry.

Ahhh. "Patricia owns the house on the other side of me?" I asked.

He picked his head up and looked at me. "Um, yeah. I thought you knew that. I've seen you talk to her."

"Yes. Of course," I mumbled. At least Toby wasn't trying to move away. "Wait, someone offered to buy her house?" I asked, finally catching up to things.

Toby was worried because he had a stalker and now someone was buying a house close to his. I had a feeling it wasn't his stalker who had put in the offer, though.

"Yeah, that's what Mrs. Dillinger said. She works at the supermarket and knows all the gossip. Anyway, you don't think it's anything, right?" he asked, looking at me.

"No, I don't think so, but I'll look into it. I have to make some calls on the emails, as well," I said. I guess there was no putting it off now—I definitely had to call Liam.

I walked over and wrapped my arms around Toby, nuzzling my nose by his ear and sniffing. He smelled so good. I wanted to lick him all over, but now wasn't the time. I leaned back and gave him a quick kiss on the lips. He looked a little shocked—no idea why—but also pleased. Humans were an odd bunch sometimes.

"I'll be in touch. And promise me you'll holler if you need anything, ok?" I demanded.

Toby flushed but nodded, and I turned and walked out before my hellhound decided that it was a good idea to bend him over the kitchen counter. Or lay him across the table. Either would work.

I made my way across to my own porch and pulled out my cell phone, heading inside as I pressed the call button for Liam's number.

"Yeah," Liam answered distractedly, keyboard clicking in the background.

"Don't you ever get off the computer? You know we have jobs to do, right? Pretty hard to send hellbound souls on from behind a desk," I teased.

I heard the clacking stop, and Liam gave a huff. "You know, I find a ton of hellbound souls through the computer. You wouldn't believe some of the depraved shit that people post…" he trailed off, keyboard clacking again.

I humphed in reply. I actually did know, and if he wanted to find his hellbound souls online as opposed to smelling them out the old fashioned way, I guess it did give him further reach. Still, it seemed like a real pain in the ass.

"Is this a social call?" Liam asked.

"Did you put in an offer on the house next to mine?" I responded, not wasting any time.

"Wait a minute, aren't I the conservative computer nerd? Would I make such a big decision without even checking out the town?" Liam joked.

Fuck. It wasn't like Liam to do something like that, but that didn't mean he hadn't told Wilder or Corbin or even that Jude hadn't done it. Still, I didn't have time for guessing games. If there was an offer and it wasn't from a hellhound, then it was something to worry about.

"Liam, I need to know if it wasn't one of us, and if it wasn't, I need the fucker who did put an offer in tracked down," I responded.

The clacking of keys stopped, and Liam asked, "Is everything ok?"

"No," I grumbled. I sat at the kitchen table and opened my laptop, holding the phone in the crook of my shoulder while I went to the emails and forwarded them to Liam. "I need you to look into what I'm sending you," I muttered as I typed.

"What? Can't hear you, Dex. Sounds like you're in a fucking tunnel. It couldn't possibly be because you've refused to join the twenty-first century and use bluetooth and instead have your phone scrunched up on your shoulder, could it?" Liam teased.

"You're a fucking hellhound. You can hear me just fine, asshole," I griped.

I heard more clicking, then Liam whistled softly. "Well shit, this isn't very pretty. I take it the original email address is your human neighbor?"

I was scanning the emails for the first time now that I'd sent them. This fucker was twisted, and I desperately wanted to go over to Toby's and… I didn't even know. I had the urge to lay over him in my hell-hound form, which was just fucking stupid, but my protective drive was beating at my skull. "Yes," I ground out, my voice guttural.

The clacking stopped again. "Dex, are you alright?" Liam asked.

All I could was growl low in my throat.

"Ok, stop reading the emails," Liam said calmly.

Everything was taking on a red haze, and my eyes were glued to the screen. I knew I was still growling, but I couldn't help it.

"Dex!" Liam shouted, and I jerked backwards, blinking a few times.

I grunted in reply.

"Stop reading the emails. Close the computer. Do it now, Dexter," Liam commanded.

I chafed at the order, but I did it anyway.

"Take a few deep breaths. Toby is safe. He's next door to you, isn't he? Is he home now?" Liam asked.

I stood up and walked over to my window, cracking it open. I listened and smelled the air. Yes, Toby was still home. Of course he was—I would have heard if he left. I could hear him puttering around the kitchen, and his smell was faint on the breeze. It also smelled like he was cooking something. Or, more accurately, burning something. I smiled despite myself.

"Yes, he's home. He's burning dinner," I commented.

"Better?" Liam asked.

"Yeah," I responded. "I just…" I trailed off, not knowing what to say. Finally I just muttered, "He feels like pack."

Liam was quiet for a moment, and I expected a million questions, but instead I just heard the clacking of keys start up again, and his voice was business-like when he responded. "Well, ok then. Let's get this stalker shit figured out so we can keep your Toby safe."

Liam was an asshole at times, and he was totally the big brother of the group, but he always had my back, and I was so thankful for that. Sometimes he really did know exactly what we all needed.

"The house offer?" I asked, wondering if that was also a loose end.

"Ah, yeah, sorry. That wasn't me, but it was the pack. Jude told Corbin about it, and Corbin did his witchy mojo shit and read some tea leaves or some such thing, and he told me about it before he put the offer in. The property is huge—it's comprised of three actual lots if we wanted to build additional structures—and there's even a fully furnished pool house in the back that would serve as an apartment for someone who needed more space," Liam replied.

We were probably both thinking of Atlas. He was the loner of the group, with good reason, and although he was pack, he liked his space, too.

"Ok, so about this stalker…" Liam started, and I grunted in reply.

He continued to chatter on about IP addresses and VPNs and other weird IT initials that made no sense to me, and I just grunted along, happy that he was looking into things.

This would probably mean that someone, whether it was Corbin, Jude, or Liam, would show up soon, but suddenly that didn't sound so bad. It would be someone extra to help me protect Toby, and that was all that was important to me at the moment.

Somehow my sweet, cute neighbor had become more important to me than I thought possible, and I didn't know what I would do if something happened to him. I pitied any fool who tried to harm him. I would burn them and everything they held dear down to protect my Toby.

CHAPTER 13

TOBY

Ok, so cooking wasn't my strong point, right along with anything involving power tools. I thought about asking Dex over for some take-out, but then I wondered if that seemed a little desperate. After all, I'd seen him a few times today already. Plus, I knew he was looking into the internet creep, and I didn't want to distract him. Or be a hassle.

I sighed, pulled out a fork, and opened the fridge, grabbing a tub of chicken salad I'd picked up at the market. I ate it with the fridge open, staring mindlessly into the void looking for something more appealing to eat.

Why was it that even when you went grocery shopping there was still nothing to eat? It was some sort of cosmic mystery that defied all logic.

I took a few more bites, put the lid on, and headed upstairs, grabbing my laptop. Unfortunately, books didn't write themselves, and I had work to do. If I was going to channel my kisses with Dex for my next few chapters, well, he'd never know. And at least in my fantasy world, I could give everyone the orgasm they deserved.

That was the great thing about books—there was never bad sex, everyone got a happily ever after, and the bad guys always got what they deserved. Was it any wonder I preferred fantasy to real life? With that, I settled in to get lost in a world where I didn't have a stalker. Ok, my main character did have a psychotic vampire after him, but I knew exactly how that would turn out.

Well, mostly, anyway. Sometimes characters had minds of their own. With that amusing thought, I settled into bed with my computer on my lap and got lost in my own world.

I woke up to banging.

I had a weird moment of total disorientation where I thought my hot vampire MC (who just so happened to look just like Dex) was pounding on the door to come in so we could have wild and crazy wall sex, but after blinking a few times I realized I was laying in bed and that had just been a dream.

That's what I got for writing into the late hours of the night and falling asleep mid-chapter. I was still just boring old me, and the banging was coming from outside, not my front door. (And there would be no crazy wall sex, which was actually way hotter in novels than in real life. At least in my experience.)

I should probably have been freaking out, but if I heard banging, I knew Dex heard it too, and I thought it had been going on for some time based on its appearance in my dream. Maybe it was stupid to have such total faith in Dex, but he said he'd protect me, and I believed him.

I grabbed my phone from my nightstand to check the time, and I realized it was after ten in the morning. So totally not too early for… whatever the hell that was.

Eventually I crawled out of bed and looked out the window.

Sexy Neighbor was on a ladder next to the giant tree in the front yard. The banging had stopped, and it looked like he was adjusting something on the tree.

I had no fucking clue what he was doing, but it was the perfect excuse to go out and chat with him. I ran into the bathroom to get myself semi-presentable. I peed, brushed my teeth (because eww, morning breath), tackled my hair into some form of submission, and ran back into the bedroom to throw on some jeans and a t-shirt.

I had a moment to ponder if I should wear something sexier, but I didn't hear banging, and I wanted to get out before Dex went back inside. Plus, it would take way too much time and brainpower to sex myself up at ten in the morning.

By the time I got outside, Dex was off the ladder, and he looked over when my front door banged open. (Maybe I was a little too enthusiastic in my exit.)

I gave an awkward wave, and Dex sauntered over, all hot muscle and sexiness. He had on a pair of black jeans and a black hoodie, but I could tell that he didn't have a shirt on underneath since it was halfway unzipped.

Holy hotness, Batman. Was I drooling? Maybe a little. Was climbing him like a tree still an option?

"Morning," he rumbled.

"Hey!" I said, giving my little wave again. I stuck my hands in my pockets before I could do something else stupid with them, like grab onto him and pull him in for a kiss. Because we weren't at that point yet. Right?

He leaned against the bottom rail on my steps while I looked down on him from my porch, and ohmygod if that didn't put dirty thoughts into my head.

Then again, with Dex, it didn't take much. Plus, apparently waking up from a sexy dream about a take charge vampire had made me more than my usual level of horny.

Dex took a deep breath in and grinned at me.

"So, uh, what are you up to?" I asked.

Because, yeah, I sucked with people. I was a very good stalker, but not so good with the actual interactions. Luckily Dex didn't seem to mind too much.

"I thought maybe some extra motion sensor lights might be helpful," he said, motioning toward the tree. "And I fixed your door frame—sorry about that—and then I did your house numbers, which I think you were working on the other day," he added, gesturing up to my front door.

I looked over, and yup, my door looked all fixed, and not only were my house numbers on securely, but they were nice large new ones. They were the same color as my old ones and looked fancy. It was so sweet that Dex had done that for me.

"I put a motion sensor light up on your porch too. I hope that's ok. I added some to my house as well. I figured a little extra security never hurts," he added, pointing to something above my head, where presumably another light was now set up.

"Wow. Thank you so much, Dex. I really, really appreciate it," I said, stepping down to look up at the light. It was affixed to my porch overhang and had two lights pointing out and a box in the center. It wasn't that big, but I thought it would be noticeable to anyone trying to sneak in. "I should probably get, like, a doorbell camera or something, I guess," I mumbled, thinking about security. It had always seemed like a waste to me, since we really didn't have any neighbors and no one was coming out this way to steal packages or anything. But it was probably a good idea.

Dex gave me a funny look, but then he nodded and said, "Yeah, I can set that up if you want."

"Yes, that would be great. I'm not the best with installing stuff," I laughed.

Dex smiled at me. God, he was sexy.

"What do I owe you for all this?" I asked.

"Nothing. It's no problem. I want to keep you safe," he said.

Aww, that was totally sweet. I figured I'd find some way to pay him back for it (and not with sex, brain—get yourself out of the gutter). I would say I'd cook for him, but maybe I'd order some takeout instead— that would be safer for everyone.

"Do you, umm, want to come in for coffee?" I asked.

He smiled and bounded up the porch, and I opened the door and led us to the kitchen. I busied myself with the coffee maker and asked, "Did you look at the emails?" I felt myself blushing and couldn't help it. They were embarrassing. Some of them were mean, and some were sexually explicit, and I knew I had no reason to feel ashamed, because I sure as hell didn't send them, but somehow I still had this nasty feeling squirming in my gut when I thought about them.

"Not all of them," he answered, watching me closely. "I don't have to if you don't want me to. I did send them on to a friend to try and analyze them, or do whatever technology magic he can, but I don't have to read the rest of them if it makes you uncomfortable."

I chuckled weakly as the coffee started sputtering, turning around to get two mugs, the sugar, and some cream from the fridge and setting them down in front of us. "No. It's ok. I know it's not my fault and all, but it still feels… I don't know. Just icky, I guess."

Dex came around from the other side of the counter, took my face between his hands, looked me in the eyes, and said, "You are not responsible for anyone else's actions, and I don't want you reading any more emails. I will take care of you, Toby. I promise."

Swoonworthy. Dex was perfect, and I couldn't help standing on my tiptoes to attack him with my mouth.

Luckily, his mouth attacked right back.

This was no gentle, flirty kiss like earlier. This was all heat and tongues dancing and lips nibbling. He held my face as our mouths pressed hungrily together, and without any thought I ran my hands up under his hoodie to feel his bare chest. He growled low in his throat, pressing closer to me.

The man was on fire. Holy smokes—pun fucking intended.

He stepped away for a half a second to rip his hoodie up over his head, then his mouth crashed down into mine again. The next breath of air had my shirt peeled off, and we were bare chest to bare chest.

I didn't even have time to feel self-conscious, because Dex was touching me everywhere. It was like he suddenly had more than two hands. His skin was hot and hard against mine, and I could feel his cock pressing against my belly. The man was fucking huge as far as I could tell. It was such a turn on that I had made him that hard just from kissing.

His mouth pressed against my neck, teeth gently nibbling, and I whimpered low in my throat, grinding my own hard cock against his leg. It felt so fucking good, and I thought I might literally come in my pants. I don't think I'd ever been so turned on from kissing someone.

Then again, up until yesterday I don't know that I'd ever kissed someone quite like Dex.

"Please," I ground out, not even really knowing what I was asking for. Whatever he wanted, I was there for it.

He nipped my neck again, his hand gently tweaking my nipple at the same time, but then his hot skin moved away from mine. I mewled out in disappointment, except he didn't move away; he moved down.

Holy fuck.

"I need to taste you," he grumbled, his voice low and growly and sexy as hell, and he was already unbuttoning and unzipping my jeans as I made sounds of agreement. He pulled my pants and boxer briefs down in one quick move, and before I could even steady myself my dick was surrounded by hot, wet suction.

I almost fucking fell over. Holy shit.

Dex reached an arm up to steady me, even as his mouth continued to work me, and I leaned against the counter behind me. When I looked down he was looking up at me, bobbing up and down on my dick. His tongue was tracing around the head, licking at the sensitive underside at a frantic pace that was about to send me over the edge. He was doing that sexy as fuck growly thing, and I felt the vibrations on my cock.

Then his mouth took my cock completely, and I could feel his throat swallowing around me, squeezing the head, wet and fiery heat surrounding my length.

The pleasure was so intense that my knees literally buckled, but Dex was there, his hand holding me up, and his fingers found their way to my nipple, giving a little tug. I cried out as he continued to suck on my cock, his tongue doing something that felt amazing but that I couldn't even explain.

When I opened my eyes again, not even realizing I had closed them, I swear to god it looked like his eyes flashed red, and that was it. I didn't have time to warn him before my orgasm was crashing into me, my legs actually shaking and my chest heaving with the intensity of it.

He sucked me gently through it, extending the pleasure, and it was like he knew exactly when to pull off. When I had my wits about me again, I looked down, and Dex's head was resting against my thigh, his chest heaving. I put a hand down and ran it through his hair, which was soft and silky and fucking beautiful.

I couldn't quite see his face, but he pressed a kiss against my thigh that made me shiver.

"Let me…" I started, but he looked up at me, and his eyes… I didn't know if I was seeing shit or if I needed my light bulbs replaced or what the fuck, but I swear that there were flames in them. Glowing red and blue flames danced in his eyes, and I opened my mouth to say more,

but nothing came out.

He blinked slowly, and when his eyes opened they were normal again. Not that Dex's eyes were really normal. They were a golden hazel color that seemed to look brown most of the time, but sometimes you could see hints of green or blue if the light hit them the right way.

"If you give me a minute, I'll totally return the favor," I whispered, mesmerized by his sexiness. Still, I managed to not sound like a complete idiot as I said it (hopefully). I didn't want him to think I was a selfish lover.

"No need," he said, chuckling lightly, and he let me slide down onto the floor, my legs incapable of holding me. He shifted me over at the last minute so I was sitting slightly to the side.

I was about to get indignant—I sure as fuck would return the favor, and I really wanted to get my mouth on his dick—only I noticed that his pants were undone and pulled slightly down.

He wasn't fully hard anymore, but his dick was still a thing of glory. He was apparently a shower and a grower, and I almost giggled at the absurd thought. It was long and thick and the prettiest pink penis I had ever seen. The head glistened wetly, and I didn't care that he wasn't fully hard. I was no schlep in the blow job department. I would get him hard. Problem solved.

I managed to look up at his face, gauging whether he just wasn't interested or was being considerate of my post-orgasm haze. He was staring at me intently, and I swear I fell a little in love with him just based on the look on his face. I don't think anyone had ever looked at me with such passion and possessiveness. I felt like I belonged to Dex, and rather than it feeling creepy, it felt really fucking good.

"I want to…" I started, but he leaned in and kissed me gently. I could taste myself faintly on his tongue, and it was hot as hell knowing he had swallowed me down.

He leaned over to whisper in my ear, "You tasted so good, and you were so fucking beautiful in your pleasure that I couldn't hold back. I promise you can return the favor next time."

He… What? I looked over then, and yep, my kitchen floor had cum on it. Holy shit. Giving me head had made him come? Well that was hot as fuck. And next time? Yes please. I was so down for next time.

I smiled stupidly at him, having no idea what to say. We were both

sitting on my kitchen floor, dicks out, and apparently it was time for my awkwardness to kick in. What did I say now? Only before I could open my mouth to say who knows what, Dex tilted his head to the side, apparently listening to something.

He stood up then, sighed, and extended a hand to me, saying, "I think we're going to have some company."

I didn't hear anything, but I took his word for it and managed to button and zip myself up while Dex did the same, both of us then getting our shirts back on. He didn't seem terribly rushed, and he grabbed paper towels to clean the floor. It was then that I heard the sound of an engine coming up the drive and the faint hum of music. It only then occurred to me to get nervous—who was visiting?

As if Dex sensed my mood, he looked at me and said, "Don't worry. They're my… people." He sighed then, grumbling something under his breath about timing.

I wasn't sure exactly what to do next. Kiss him goodbye? Ask him to text me? I put my hand up, ready to do something stupid with it, I'm sure, but he grabbed it and pulled me toward the front door.

Well, I guess I was about to meet some of Dex's people, whatever that odd phrase meant. Friends? Family? Fellow serial killers? I guess I would find out.

Chapter 14

Dexter

Leave it to pack to show up at the most inconvenient times. Although I supposed they could have shown up when Toby was down my throat, and then I might've actually killed them.

Toby had been so sexy, so responsive, that I hadn't been able to help touching myself. When I'd tasted him, my own orgasm had rushed through me, and my hellhound had been perilously close to the surface. I had the urge to devour him, to have him under me, submitting in the most sensual way possible. I wanted to be inside him in every way imaginable, causing him to make those sexy little sounds while I filled him up with my seed.

I supposed it was good I'd heard the faint sound of the car engine and the music, otherwise I wasn't even sure what I would have done. My instincts seemed to be taking over with Toby, and I didn't want to scare my pretty human.

As I grabbed his hand and led the way outside, I came to the conclusion that I was keeping Toby. Permanently.

I nodded to myself as that decision was made. I pondered for a moment whether that would be agreeable with Toby. He liked me. I turned him on. He liked his orgasm. He wanted to "return the favor" (like it

had been a favor and not a magnificent treat). He trusted me.

It would be fine. I would just have to… not move too fast. Humans were weird about dating and stuff like that.

They had inconveniently short life spans, too, but Corbin might be able to help with that. And Jude would be able to help me navigate the whole human thing. I didn't think it was a coincidence that those were the two packmates who were currently pulling into my driveway, either. I heard Toby humming along to the Beatles song Jude was playing, and I almost smiled. At least they could bond over music.

I pulled Toby close and tucked him under my arm as Jude shut the car off and his music stopped. I heard Corbin muttering, "Blackbirds are not corvids."

Jude just happily laughed, both of them turning toward Toby's porch and walking over. I suddenly felt a spark of protectiveness, and I sized up my packmates. Jude was slightly shorter than me, and his curly, light hair and easy smile made him seem more like a puppy than a hellhound. Corbin's long, dark hair was up in some kind of man-bun, and he was slightly taller than both Jude and I. They were both muscular and fit, and they were probably considered sexy by others. They certainly seemed to draw both men and women to them.

Would Toby think they were sexy? I gripped Toby tighter, a low, subvocal growl emanating from my chest before I could stop it.

Both Corbin and Jude stopped walking, and I heard cawing from the trees. Corbin looked up at the crows and ravens that were, of course, perched there. They hadn't been there earlier. Jude elbowed him in the side, though, before Corbin could do anything witchy, then he smiled at me.

"Hey Dex! Gonna introduce us to your… friend?" Jude called out, emphasizing that Toby was mine.

It seemed to calm something in me, but Jude's hesitation must have made Toby nervous, because I felt him tense up. I shook myself a bit. Jude and Corbin were pack. They were friends. They wouldn't steal Toby away or hurt him. They would help protect Toby.

And now I'd gone and fucked things up. I could sense Toby's unease and… insecurity, maybe? I looked down at him, but he wouldn't look at me, and he tried to pull away from under my arm. I wasn't letting him go, though. Jude and Corbin observed the slightly awkward wrangling

that ensued as I tried to grip him tighter and he tried to wiggle away. Jude looked like he was trying not to laugh, and Corbin had his head tilted inquisitively.

"He's my boyfriend," I blurted out, and at least Toby stopped struggling to be free from under my arm. In fact, he put a hand on my chest and looked up at me, his mouth slightly open in surprise.

I hadn't called him my mate or anything. Hopefully boyfriend was an acceptable human term. I had swallowed his seed—didn't that make us boyfriends? It's not like I did that with just anyone. I'd also placed cameras all around the outside of his house to protect him. Not that he knew about that, though. Huh. Maybe I should tell him. Was that sweet or weird? I thought it was sweet, but humans were prickly things.

Jude would probably know.

Toby still hadn't said anything, though, and now I was getting nervous. I didn't sense that he was upset. He just looked… shocked.

Jude finally did laugh then, and he bounded up the steps, hand extended to shake Toby's hand. Corbin followed slowly behind, looking up into the trees again where the crows and ravens were watching.

"Nice to meet you, Dex's boyfriend," Jude said, smiling his puppy dog smile.

I resisted growling when their hands touched. Barely. Corbin wisely only nodded his head at Toby.

"Toby. It's nice to meet you too," he said, and then both Jude and Toby stared at me.

Fuck. I was supposed to be doing something, wasn't I? I had no fucking clue what, though. Human manners and all that were Jude's thing. He'd been the one to grow up with them, after all. Corbin was certainly not going to be any help. He was staring off into the trees rather than paying us any mind, and I thought he was subtly scenting things as well.

Jude cleared his throat, finally saying, "We're… friends of Dexter's."

Even I knew that sounded suspicious.

"Brothers," Corbin said, finally looking over at Toby and inhaling deeply. "This is a good place," he commented.

Jude rolled his eyes. "Yeah, I guess you could say we're brothers. I'm stuck with these two socially inept weirdos whether I want to be or not. We all grew up together as family."

It must have been the right thing to say, because Toby laughed and seemed to relax against me.

"I don't know too much about Dex's family, but it's great to meet you," Toby said softly.

"There's a few more of us, but we're the only two you'll have to put up with for now," Jude smiled.

"You guys want to come in and have some tea?" Toby asked politely.

Jude looked like he was about to accept, but Corbin cut in. "You have friends who visit you?" he asked. "Two of them?"

Jude elbowed him, and he grunted and gave him a dirty look.

"Yeah, his friends were just here the other night," I answered.

Corbin nodded, then he focused on Toby, reaching his hand out for a handshake. Jude and I were both kinda shocked—Corbin didn't often touch humans—but Toby gamely shook his hand. Corbin nodded once, said, "Welcome to the family, Toby," and then turned around and walked off toward my house.

And I thought I was bad at dealing with humans.

Jude laughed though, saying, "There Corbin goes proving my point. I'm Jude, by the way, and although tea sounds great, Corbin probably wants to check out the house first, and we need to get settled in. We'll definitely take a rain check, though. It's really great to meet you. Maybe you can come over to Dexter's tomorrow for lunch and we can all get to know each other. As long as you don't mind socially awkward people," he joked.

"I'm a hermit writer. I'm the definition of socially awkward," Toby joked back, and Jude laughed easily.

I wasn't usually jealous of Jude's ability to get along with humans, but I hugged Toby closer to me at his chuckle. I wanted to be the one to make him chuckle. Toby casually put a hand on my chest again, almost like he was comforting me, and I practically rumbled in happiness at the touch.

Jude smiled and then turned to go, calling out, "We'll see you to-morrow, Toby!"

He was down the steps and heading after Corbin, who was making his way around my house and toward the property on the other side. Trees and distance made it hard to see—at least for humans—but Corbin would find it just fine.

"Umm, they're passing by your house," Toby said.

I looked down at him, unable to resist giving him a kiss on the lips. He looked bemused at that.

"Boyfriends, huh?" he asked.

"Is that ok?" I asked back, not that I was sure what I would do if he said no. I could woo him, though. I'm sure I could figure that out. I didn't think tying him up in my bedroom was a good alternative, although it did briefly occur to me. It would solve the stalker problem, too, if he was always attached to me. But humans liked having their space, unfortunately.

"Yeah," he murmured, blushing. "That's great. Do you want me to come over tomorrow?"

"Of course I do. I always want you to come over, Toby," I responded.

"And those are your… brothers?" he asked.

I could tell he would drop it if I didn't want to answer questions. While I couldn't tell him everything, at least not yet, I certainly wanted him to have some details.

"Yeah," I answered. "We were all raised by a guy named Wilder. Some of us had family but didn't fit in, and some of us lost our parents, but we formed a… family, I guess, and we've been close since we were kids."

I almost told Toby we'd formed a pack, but that wasn't human-speak.

"They seem nice," Toby said.

"Jude seems nice, and Corbin is weird," I responded.

Toby chuckled at that. "Yeah, although I think he was distracted by all the birds. I swear we don't usually have so many crows around. It's kind of cool."

I smiled. I was glad Toby thought so, because they weren't going anywhere with Corbin around. He had an affinity for corvids, and Toby would see that before too long. I almost couldn't wait to eavesdrop on his next conversation with his friends to see what supernatural story he came up with for Corbin.

Speaking of stories… "You going to go do some writing today? Or do you need to run errands?" I asked.

"Writing for me," Toby sighed. "And I really do need to get to it. I'm on a deadline, and I got a little derailed by those emails. Is one of your brothers the one who is looking into it?"

"Yeah, Liam is, but he isn't here. He'll do what he can, though, and I'll let you know. What scene are you working on now?" I asked. If Toby needed more inspiration, I was sure I could provide some.

He blushed, though, mumbling something about his MCs reuniting. I figured that might mean a sex scene, so I leaned down and kissed him again. By the time I pulled back we were both breathing heavily. I gave him a wink, hopped off the porch, and sauntered over to my place to go inside.

I heard him mutter, "So sexy," and I tried not to strut too much when I walked inside.

I barely had time to get a glass of water before Jude and Corbin were coming in. Corbin, of course, had a fucking crow on his shoulder.

"He better not shit in my house," I grumbled.

Corbin smiled. "They only shit on your stuff at the compound because you kept eating the peanuts I left out for them. I told you they hold grudges."

Yeah, they sure as fuck did. Jude got pretty stones and baubles dropped at his feet and I got shit on for a week until I made it up to them. Vindictive little fuckers. It sort of made me respect them more.

New crows, new opportunities, though. I'd have to start leaving treats out and make nice with Corbin's new friends. I also realized they'd be a great warning sign for Toby.

"They'll let us know if anyone is coming, right? An early alarm system?" I asked.

"Of course," Corbin replied.

"Liam told us about Toby's stalker," Jude answered. "We'll work together to protect him for you."

"This is a good place," Corbin reiterated. Jude and I both looked at him. Corbin was… odd, even by hellhound standards. His mother had been a witch, and he'd obviously gotten a lot of her traits. What he said also carried weight because of it.

"We checked out the house," Jude added. "The current owner is a sweet old lady who was happy to let us look around. She's already in the process of organizing her stuff to move. She's going to hire people to clean it all out and asked if we wanted to keep furniture or anything. She thinks she can be out in a month. She's excited to move."

"You think this will work for a new pack central location?" I asked.

"Yes," Corbin answered.

"You're right—it feels good here," Jude added. "And we didn't smell any rot in town, but there's plenty of cities nearby to go hunting. Of course we won't all always stay here, either, but it'll be a good home base. I think we should run the perimeter of town anyway, though. I think you probably need to get out, too."

I knew Jude meant in our hellhound form, which we rarely did, but he was right—I did need to let my hellhound out. It would be good to run with pack, too.

I showed Jude and Corbin up to two of the guest bedrooms and let them get settled in, and the afternoon passed with us catching up and exchanging stories. They both rolled their eyes when I told them my stray human story, but thankfully I didn't get any lectures like I had from Liam. Jude had apparently been traveling around and doing city sweeps, and Corbin had been hunting down outliers in smaller villages and urban areas. He had a gift for sensing where to go beyond even just scenting a rotting soul.

By the time night rolled around, we were all itching to get out, and when the last bits of daylight had faded, we all headed out the back door, in sync on running as our hellhounds. Jude and Corbin started to strip, but I took a moment to look over at Toby's house, breathing in deeply. His downstairs light was on, and all was quiet. I stripped out of my clothes, my eyes on his windows, hoping for a glimpse of him.

I let my hellhound form out, shaking myself out and looking over at my packmates. They were grinning their hellhound grins, flames lightly emanating from their dark fur coats. Jude was the first to bound off into the night, and Corbin and I followed, running through the forest and occasionally bumping into one another playfully.

We made a full circuit of the town in very little time—our hellhound forms were even faster than our human forms, but it wasn't long before I was ready to head back. Corbin gave a little huff at me as I broke away, and Jude gave a low, eerie howl that I knew would probably freak out anyone close enough to hear. I simply chuffed at them and turned to race back toward home.

I was called to Toby, and I wanted to be close to him. Surely a little peek in his window wouldn't hurt.

CHAPTER 15

TOBY

I was pulled from my writing by the distant howl of… I didn't even know. It didn't sound like a dog or a wolf. It was kind of eerie, but in a cool way. I moved my laptop to the side and stood up, stretching. I think my back cracked in about eight places. Writing sitting on the couch probably wasn't the best spot, but I felt more comfy there than at my desk.

Not that I'd only been writing. There were promos to make, a website to update, a newsletter to send out… and email to check. Although I hadn't done that. I was letting Amy take care of the email for now, and I had sent her Dex's email address so she could just forward any emails to him. So far, there hadn't been anything. I wasn't sure whether to be nervous or thankful about that. Maybe the guy had just given up?

I wandered over to the window in my living room, looking out into the night. Dex's front light was on, but I didn't see any movement in his window. I'm sure he was catching up with his brothers.

I had been a little jealous when I'd first seen them, I had to admit. They were fucking hot. They were both built similar to Dex, and I was definitely not the definition of a perfect body. Dex didn't seem to have any complaints, and I hadn't felt self-conscious when I was with him, but being faced with two such sexy friends right after our moment had been a little awkward.

The weird pause before Jude had said friends had totally made me wonder if they were more than friends. I had no idea what Dex's dating life was like. Or hook-up life. But he hadn't seemed to want to let me go, and I admit I was still a little giddy that he'd called me his boyfriend. I wouldn't have labeled us that yet—we hadn't even gone on a date—but I wasn't going to complain. I mean, we were neighbors and chatted all the time, and I knew if I asked for a date, Dex would totally give me one. He was so sweet.

And apparently he had grown up in some kind of foster care situation. I didn't want to push and ask too many questions, but I thought his quirky ways (not that I was one to talk) totally made more sense now. He'd obviously found a family of similar "brothers," joined the military or something like that because it gave him structure (even if he tortured people or whatever), and now was settling down for a quiet life in the country. Only maybe the government still occasionally called on him to take care of things, which was why he was out at all hours of the night.

Yeah, I was backstorying again—perils of being a writer.

I moved away from the window, obviously not able to get a glimpse of Dex or his sexy as fuck brothers, and decided to give Josh a call.

He picked up on the first ring, and he sounded… tired when he answered. I was worried about him.

"Hey! What's cooking?" I asked.

"Hopefully not you, because we all know how that turns out," he joked.

At least he could still joke around. "Hardy har, Josh. Seriously, you sound tired. All ok?"

Josh gave a grunt. "Yeah. I've got some shit going on, but I'm ok. I'm sorting it out."

"You need any help? You know Sebbie and I are always here for you," I responded.

His voice softened. "I know. And I'll fill you guys in. It's just… a lot right now. I'd rather talk about something else. So distract me, literary genius. Is the little old lady in the other house really a witch? Or a harpy? Something good, I'm sure," he joked.

"Patricia?" I asked, playing along. I thought about it for a second and hummed. "Nah, she's totally a vampire. I don't think she's aged at all since I moved in."

"But she's old! Aren't vampires all young and sexy?" Josh joked.

"Nah, they're the best versions of themselves at whatever age they were turned. And she's in great shape for an older lady. She's probably selling her house because we'll all start to notice soon that she doesn't age," I answered, playing around.

"She's selling? Really? Does she have a buyer?" Josh asked.

I thought about filling him in on the stalker situation, but Josh seemed to need light and fun right now, and I didn't want to worry him with that shit. "She does, apparently. Although I don't know who," I answered.

It occurred to me then that Dex seemed like he did know, and his brothers had walked past his house initially, over towards Patricia's house. Huh. I wondered if his family was buying the house next door? That would be pretty cool, I guess.

"Dex has two hot as fuck sort of brothers," I said. The train of thought totally made sense in my head, and Josh was used to my conversational leaps, because he just went along with it.

"Oh yeah? Are they serial killers, too?" he joked.

"Nah," I answered, heading out toward the back porch. It looked like a nice night, and I could use a little fresh air. I opened the back door and stood on the back step overlooking the forest as I chatted with Josh. "The one is way too sweet to be a serial killer. He's all curly-haired golden boy. I bet he's got some crazy magical power like teleportation or something. Maybe a super powerful warlock who everyone underestimates."

Josh chuckled. "And I bet he's cute."

"Absolutely," I answered.

"Of course," Josh agreed lightly.

"The other brother is dark and mysterious, and he kept looking up at the trees. I'm going with shifter for him. Or thunderbird, maybe. Oh, maybe a dragon. Yeah, I'll definitely go with dragon. He's also sexy as hell," I laughed.

I heard a low rumble off in the woods as I added, "But Dex is way sexier, of course."

I heard a chuff from the woods, and I wondered what the heck was out there. We didn't usually have wolves or bears out here, but I guess we could. I backed up toward my door a little bit, suddenly feeling nervous.

"I think there's an animal in my yard," I whispered to Josh.

"Well, yeah Toby, I'm sure there is. You live backed up to protected forest land. I'm sure there's a lot of animals in your yard," Josh said, and he totally had his you're letting your imagination run away with you voice on.

"I mean, I think there's a big animal in my yard," I whispered.

"Well, go inside," he said.

"Pfft. Like I'd do something so reasonable," I answered. I heard a door slam in the background at Josh's and a strident voice call out. Sounded like his dickhead boyfriend was there, and I hadn't even gotten a chance to fill Josh in on my new boyfriend status or my sexual escapades.

Josh gave a sigh. "I gotta go, Toby. I'll fill you in later this week, ok?"

"Sure. You sure you're ok?" I asked.

"I will be," he answered cryptically, and with that, we said our good-byes and hung up.

Was it wrong that I hoped they were breaking up? Because I totally did. His boyfriend was an asshole. With that thought, I reached for the door and opened it, but rather than go inside, I reached in and shut off the back porch light. Aside from attracting bugs, it didn't make looking into the woods easy. I really did have the feeling that something big was out there.

I felt like I was being watched, but I wasn't particularly worried—Dex was next door, and if I screamed he'd hear me. Plus, I was a half a step from my back door, and I figured I could get inside before any-thing could get me. It wasn't like there were cheetahs roaming around these parts. Coyotes, bears, or wolves? Maybe, and it would be pretty cool to spot one. It was probably just a buck, though. We got deer around here all the time.

As my eyes adjusted to the light, I thought I saw something glowing faintly off in the trees. I rubbed my eyes and took a step forward. The glow looked… red? And blue? The red could be from a reflection of light on animal eyes, I guess. I mean red eye was a thing in pictures for a reason, wasn't it? Although it seemed like animal eyes usually glowed yellow. But the blue was weird. I took another step forward and down the first step of my back porch.

That was… what the fuck was that? It was pitch black and blended in really well, except I swore there were licks of red and blue dancing along its fur. I got a sense of something really large. It was easily bear sized, only it wasn't shaped like a bear. It seemed to be laying down and shaped more like a wolf, only wolves did not get that big. I could make out eyes staring straight at me.

"Holy fuck, you're huge," I whispered. "What are you?"

It shifted the tiniest bit, but it stayed laying down, watching me. I swear its eyes were focused right on me. And they were definitely glowing. The thing looked like it was straight out of one of my books. I was almost afraid to blink in case it disappeared when I did.

I took another step down, which was probably stupid, and the creature—whatever it was—cocked its head, but it stayed laying down.

"You're beautiful," I murmured. "I think I'm hallucinating," I added after that.

The beast's mouth opened, and it started to rise, and that's when I realized that I was off my steps and not terribly close to my back door. I had a total oh shit moment and stumbled backwards, running into my steps in the process and falling hard on my ass.

It only took a second, and I should have been scared out of my mind that the thing was going to come at me, but when I looked up, it was gone.

Well fuck. I rubbed my eyes and stood up, scanning the woods, but they were empty. I eventually went in my back door, wondering what the hell had just happened. Had I imagined it? I mean, yeah, I had a vivid imagination, but I didn't usually hallucinate things. I was a lucid dreamer, but I was wide awake. Maybe I was just way more tired than I thought I was, and I had been really stressed out.

I walked into the kitchen, leaning against my kitchen island. It felt sort of weird against my back though, and I turned around to look at it. There were two dents in the countertop. I didn't know what the hell the counter was made of, but I knew it wasn't flimsy. How the hell had it gotten dents in it?

"Toby, you're losing it. Imagining shit and everything," I muttered to myself.

At that moment, though, I heard an eerie howl off in the night once again.

I should've felt nervous, I knew that logically, but suddenly I was just really tired, and I felt… protected. Maybe it was crazy, but if there were wild animals in the woods, it would make it that much harder for anyone to sneak up on me.

I'd have to let Dex know tomorrow, though.

The last thing I wanted was Sexy Neighbor to get eaten by the local werewolf (unless he was the local werewolf, in which case—lucky me).

With that thought, and probably more calm than I should have felt considering something weird was outside, I headed up to bed. I had a feeling I'd have some pretty good dreams, and I looked forward to falling asleep imagining a sexy werewolf and an unassuming human finding a love match. You never knew when new book ideas would pop up.

As I drifted off to sleep, I thought about those eyes again. Something niggled at me, but I was too sleepy to get a grasp on it, and I drifted off with them glowing in my mind.

I woke to the sound of cawing.

Like, a lot of cawing. I hopped out of bed and ran to the window. The trees were filled with black birds. I was guessing crows, although some looked too large to be crows. Probably ravens—Sebbie liked feeding the birds and he had ravens that hung around by his property, so I knew they were way bigger.

I didn't know what the hell they were cawing about, but I saw Corbin step off the front porch. A few flew down and one even landed on the guy's shoulder.

Like that was perfectly normal and not weird as fuck.

Jude and Dex followed him outside, and at that point I made out the shape of a van coming up the long drive. I expected it to veer off toward Paricia's property, although it didn't quite look like a moving van. Only it didn't—it kept coming until it was in my driveway.

Shit. I hadn't ordered something, had I? I didn't think I had a delivery coming, but maybe I'd forgotten something? I figured no one would steal it with those three outside, so I went and hopped into the shower before I went down to see what I'd forgotten. No point heading out there all disheveled. After all, I had a boyfriend to impress now. I grinned to myself at the thought.

If luck was with me, maybe I'd find Sexy Neighbor and his sexy brothers lounging on their porch when I picked up my package.

A guy could always hope, and as unlucky as stalker dude had been, I felt like my luck was definitely changing with the new boyfriend development.

CHAPTER 16

DEXTER

"Your human saw you," Corbin said when he meandered downstairs in the morning.

I stared at the crow on his shoulder. "Tattletale," I muttered.

It cawed and then flew out the open window. I really hoped it didn't understand me, because I did not want to get shit on again. I sighed and started ruffling through my cabinets for an appropriate offering to the birds.

Jude bounded into the kitchen humming under his breath.

"He does not think I'm a walrus," I complained.

Jude laughed. "What did he think, then? Did you tell him?"

"He thinks I'm a werewolf," I chuckled. "Or that he was hallucinating."

Corbin smirked, and Jude gave an indignant growl. "Werewolf. Hah. We are so much better than freaking werewolves."

I was about to reply when Corbin's birds started making a fuss outside. Corbin was up and out before Jude and I, but we followed closely behind.

"Van coming up the driveway," Corbin muttered. "Delivery, looks like."

Jude and I both spotted it in the distance then as well. A white delivery van. Not at all suspicious or anything. Sure.

We all stood outside waiting, and when it turned into Toby's driveway, I was the first to start walking over there. I looked up at his house, but his bedroom curtain was drawn. I thought I heard footsteps, and then the sound of pipes groaning. Good—he was probably hopping in the shower or washing up. That would give us time to investigate before he came down.

You could never be too paranoid.

The delivery guy smelled fine—not a bit of rot on his soul—but he was only the messenger.

"Oh, hey!" the guy replied, getting out of the van. Really, he was more of a teenager. "I've got a delivery for this address," he said, pausing as he hauled out a colorful bouquet of flowers from the van's side door.

I growled a little as the flowers came out. Yes, they smelled like flowers, but underneath that was something… metallic? And rotten.

Jude grabbed the flowers and Corbin had the kid pressed against the side of the van before he could blink. I looked up at Toby's house again, and his window curtain remained drawn. Good.

"Umm…" the kid said. He looked more surprised than nervous as Corbin let him up but stayed in front of him so he couldn't take the flowers back. Jude was reading the card.

"It's for Toby, no signature—just a congrats on your newest release message," Jude said.

We all looked at the kid, who apparently had some common sense, because he was starting to shift from foot to foot nervously.

"Where are you delivering from?" I asked.

"Flowers and Beyond. From Denworth," the kid answered.

"Isn't that right outside the city? Maybe a forty minute drive?" Jude asked. He'd obviously studied the area.

"Um, yeah," the kid answered, looking between us and settling on Jude. He was probably the least scary, so I let him take over on asking questions.

"Kind of far to make a flower delivery. Aren't those things usually sent to the local florist for delivery?" Jude asked.

"Yeah, I guess so, but the big boss said this was a special delivery," the kid answered. He seemed to get some sort of clue then, because he started panicking. "Is this, like, trouble or something? Are you guys, like, FBI or DEA or something? I swear it's just supposed to be flowers. I'm not, like, a drug runner or something. I didn't check the flowers or the vase, because that's not my job. I'm just a delivery guy!"

He was getting frantic, and Jude placed a hand on his shoulder while Corbin took the flowers and walked off toward the woods. Jude waited until he was out of sight before saying. "Of course you're not a drug runner. Relax. We just have some questions for you, and then you can be on your way. You're not who we're interested in."

Good. Jude let the kid think we were official. That made things so much easier. He wasn't lying, either. He was a good soul, and we weren't interested in him. If he knew what was best, he wouldn't keep making "special" deliveries for his "big boss" though.

"Which boss asked you to make this delivery?" I asked.

"Kurt. Ugh, I don't know his last name. Mandy is the manager and I usually work for her, but Kurt is the owner and stops in sometimes and has special deliveries. I swear it's always flowers and gift baskets and stuff," the kid answered.

"Maybe you should find another line of work," I suggested.

The kid nodded his head vigorously.

"Don't repeat any of this. Don't say anything to Kurt or Mandy or anyone else at work. If you decide to go work elsewhere, which might be in your best interest, just tell them you got a better offer," Jude suggested.

"Like, when should I quit?" the kid asked, eyes wide.

"Now," I answered, and Jude gave me a look.

What? I wasn't gonna waste time. The kid nodded his head nervously. "My grandma is sick. I should go visit her," he said, looking at us.

I nodded my head. Jude took out his wallet and peeled off a few bills. The kid held his hands up, like he wasn't willing to take it.

"A tip for your long delivery," Jude answered, pushing the money into his shirt pocket. I knew it would be enough to help the kid out.

The kid stared at us, as if he was unsure what to do next.

"Off with you," I finally grumbled.

That seemed to do the trick, and the kid hopped into the van and practically peeled out of the driveway. We watched him go, then turned our attention to the woods. We started walking to find Corbin and the flowers.

"Flowers and Beyond," Jude mumbled.

When we got to Corbin, who had stayed well out of sight and hearing range, I could still smell the slight rot on the flowers. A hellbound soul had handled them recently, and for quite a long time for the smell to remain. Beneath that was the odd non-flowery smell. Corbin had dismantled the flowers and held up what he'd found.

There were two listening devices painted to match the leaves they were attached to. There were also three cameras made to match the decorative stones that filled the bottom of the vase. Corbin had been holding them in his closed hand so they couldn't record anything, and after he showed us, he engulfed them in flame, destroying them.

They'd have gotten a bit of footage and sound, but Corbin would have been careful, and if we were lucky, the guy would just assume a malfunction or a range issue.

I was growling low in my throat and couldn't seem to stop. Someone had tried to spy on Toby. His stalker was the most likely candidate, and obviously the asshole knew where he lived. That definitely complicated matters.

"I'm going to destroy this Kurt," I snarled.

Corbin patted my shoulder and said, "Wait until dark when the kid is done working."

"We'll watch over your Toby, unless you'd like some assistance," Jude added, grinning. As tempting as it was, I would rather have the two of them here to keep watch, so I shook my head.

"I have to see him," I rumbled.

"You have to get yourself under control first," Jude replied.

"I have to see he's safe," I growled, and with that, I loped off toward his house.

As I climbed his steps, I took a few deep breaths, getting myself under control before I knocked on the door. I wasn't sure I was totally successful. My hellhound was a burn against my skin. Toby was in danger. Someone had tried to listen in on him and watch him. They had tried to invade his space and his home.

I had the stray thought that I would have done the exact same thing—I still would microchip him if I thought I could manage it—but that was totally different. Toby liked me, after all. We were boyfriends now. He had agreed to it.

That thought seemed to ease my hellhound a bit, and Toby opened the door at that moment.

He was freshly showered, his hair still damp, and he'd apparently hastily thrown on a t-shirt and sweatpants. He smiled at me, but that faded as I smelled his lust on the air. I moved forward until we were both inside, shutting the door behind me.

I suddenly understood the human fascination with sweatpants. As I unashamedly watched, his cock grew thicker through the fabric. I growled, fascinated, as it twitched at the sound.

I looked up, and Toby was staring at me, heat in his eyes. I don't know who moved first, but our lips crashed together. Hells, he tasted so fucking good. I nipped at his lip, making him groan in pleasure.

I moved him up against the wall and lifted him up so our cocks were lined up, grinding them together as our mouths slanted against each other.

He pulled away from my lips, crying out, "Dex!"

"What, baby? What do you want? Tell me," I murmured. "Any-thing." Then I nipped at his neck. I wanted to bite down, to mark him with my teeth. I wanted to cover him with my cum. I wanted my scent covering him so everyone would know that he was mine.

I growled again, unable to help it, barely reining in my impulses. Toby whimpered, the scent of his arousal nearly overpowering my senses.

I set him down, dragging his shirt off and his sweatpants down. Fuck, he wasn't even wearing underwear. I pulled my own shirt over my head but only had patience to unbutton my pants and pull my own cock out. I picked him back up, grabbing Toby's ass in my hands and pressing his back against the wall. I lined our cocks up against each other, and he grabbed onto my shoulders, his hands digging in.

"Holy fuck, Dex," he groaned, laying his head back against the wall and panting. His legs were wrapped around me and his hips were mak-ing little thrusts against me, our cocks bumping into each other.

It wasn't enough. I held one hand under his ass and used the other to grab both our dicks in my grip. I leaned into his neck, smelling him.

His skin was clean and soft, but underneath the soap smell I smelled the musk of Toby. It was like the forest after a rain—fresh and clean and just fucking good. His soul had not an ounce of rot on it. He was pure bliss, and I breathed him in like I could make his scent a part of me.

Our cocks were slick with precum, and I held them together and rubbed my hand up and down, gathering more precum at each pass of the heads.

"Fuck, Dex. Fuck," Toby panted. "That's too fucking good," he moaned.

I kissed him again, my tongue darting into his mouth to lick at him, sweetness with a hint of spice in his taste. His tongue traced against mine as he groaned.

I wanted to devour him.

My hand moved faster against our cocks, his mewling sounds only driving me on. I broke away from our kiss and leaned into his neck again, biting down where his neck met his shoulder.

"Holy fuck, Dex!" he cried out, and I felt his cum spattering us both. I growled as my own orgasm rushed through me, and the thought of our cum mixing together on our skin made me spurt again.

The pleasure rolled through me, and only when Toby stopped twitching in my hand did I lower us both gently to sit on the floor. Toby crawled into my lap, leaning his head against my chest, and I wrapped my arms tightly around him.

We sat like that for a moment before Toby gave a light chuckle. "Guess I'll need another shower," he murmured.

"Don't," I rumbled.

He looked up, and his eyes flared at whatever he saw on my face.

"Yeah? You going all caveman on me?" he asked.

I grunted in response, then I grabbed my shirt to give us both a wipe down. There—no sticky cum, but still the nice scent of our mixed pleasure. I raised an eyebrow at him in question.

"Thank you," he murmured, and then he gently leaned in and kissed me.

I kissed him back, laying back and pulling him on top of me so he wasn't resting on the hard floor. Our legs were intertwined, and he pulled back from the kiss and rested his head on my chest.

We snuggled like that, laying on the hardwood floor of his entryway. My chest rumbled in contentment, and I had a moment where I realized perhaps that wasn't the most human thing to do, but Toby only sighed happily and nestled closer.

My Toby was perfect. I wondered idly if it was too soon to ask him to move in with me. I supposed that was a question for Jude—he knew about human conventions. In the meantime, he could get to know Jude and Corbin today, and then later I would get to torture a flower shop owner for information and hopefully find and kill Toby's stalker.

I smiled happily as I smoothed my hand down Toby's arm. Life was good.

CHAPTER 17

So, yeah, apparently wall sex wasn't just for books.

Dex was fucking strong, though. Holy shit. Like I still wasn't sure how that had been physically possible. I knew he had muscles, but day-um.

I roused from my stupor enough to realize that I was literally sprawled on top of the man, and he was laying on my floor. "That can't be comfortable," I murmured, starting to lift myself up.

His hands only gripped me tighter, and he rumbled, "It's fine. Laying on the ground has never bothered me."

I leaned up and looked at him then, feeling sad thinking about him lying on a cold floor. The slight rumbling that I had felt underneath me seemed to stop. I swear, I felt like he had been purring, which was slightly insane.

"I want you comfortable," I said, staring down at him. God, his eyes were beautiful.

"I'm comfortable as long as you are," he rumbled, and I almost melted into a puddle of goo. How was I so fucking lucky that he had decided to be interested in me? Not that I was, like, totally lacking in self-esteem or anything. I was a kick-ass writer. I had friends. I was fun.

I gave damn good head, too. I was good boyfriend material, although I occasionally got lost in my own fantasy world.

But Dex—well, obviously he was hot as hell, and I felt lucky that we got to fool around. But he was fucking sweet, too. Of course I'd always been attracted to his sexy exterior, but there had always been something about his badass vibes combined with his slight awkwardness that was totally endearing. Then he went and did shit like say he was gonna protect me, and he fixed my house numbers and put up lights and said we were boyfriends, then he ravaged me in my hallway, cleaned me up, and snuggled me.

And then had the nerve to say that he was comfortable as long as I was comfortable.

Fuck.

I was not going to recover from him.

"What's wrong?" he asked, gently rubbing his hand up and down my back.

"You're just too good, you know that?" I answered.

"I'm really not, Toby," he said seriously.

"Pfft," I muttered. "You're good in all the ways that count. No one is perfect. I know that, despite the fact that I write books with romance."

He rumbled some form of agreement, and I felt like he wanted to argue with me more, but he settled on saying, "I'll be perfect for you, Toby. You just tell me what you need."

I looked up at him again, resting my chin on his chest. He didn't even complain about my pointy ass chin digging into him. "I'm not perfect either, you know. I make up backstories for everything. I get lost in my imagination. I suck at home improvement and cooking."

He only smiled. "I like your imagination. And I can cook and do home improvement."

I pecked him on the lips then got up, and he hesitantly let me go. He got up too, and we both gathered our clothes. Well, I gathered my clothes, and he grabbed his shirt.

"I want…" I paused, unsure how to continue. "I want you to be yourself. It won't work if you don't. I've had enough relationships to know that."

Because I did want a relationship with Dex, and he seemed to want one too. Maybe things were moving quickly, but we'd been neighbors for months before this. It wasn't like I just met the guy a week ago.

He nodded, kissing me on the lips again and grabbing my hand, his shirt in his other hand. I felt like he was ready to lead me out of the house, but hello—still naked here.

"Umm, did you still want to do lunch and have me hang with your brothers?" I asked. "You guys are welcome here, or I can go there, but I do need to get dressed," I joked.

Dex gave a low growl, looking at my body with heat in his gaze. I was so here for that rumbly, sexy sound he made.

Focus, Toby. Food. His guests.

I waited, and he apparently got himself under control, because he answered, "You want to come over? We have food and can make brunch."

I flushed, because, yeah, I probably didn't have much in the way of food, and no one wanted me cooking. I nodded then, asking, "When do you want me?"

Dex growled again. "Always, Toby. I always want you."

Fuck. He was gonna kill me with sweetness. I was not gonna survive this man.

I promised to be over in an hour or so, and I did not shower again after Dex left. I thought he would have happily had me go over right at that moment, but I had a few author things to take care of. I wasn't going to get any writing done, but I did need to catch up with my cover designer and check in with Amy. I also needed to get dressed and look presentable. Sure, Dex had seen me in pajamas and sweats and nothing at all, but I could still make a good impression.

Yesterday I didn't even know what to call him, and today I was meeting my boyfriend's family. Well, I'd met them already, but this was, like, really meeting them. I tried to take a deep breath. Dex liked me. Dex was sweet. His brothers seemed nice. Everything was fine.

With that thought, I stepped out my door. I realized as I did so that there wasn't a package on my porch. Huh. Dex hadn't brought anything in with him when he'd knocked on the door, either. I wonder what the deal had been with the truck? I'd have to ask Dex.

I walked over, nervously thinking about what I was gonna say. I might have been mumbling a bit to myself, and I flushed when the front door opened before I even made it up the last step.

"Toby!" Dex called, coming over, grabbing my hands, and kissing my forehead.

Fucking.

Swoon.

Worthy.

He led me into the house, where Jude was perched on a kitchen island stool and Corbin was working over the stove. I looked around. His house had a pretty similar layout to mine, which made sense since they were built at the same time. I think Patricia's house had been the original one on the property, and the first owner had sold off chunks of land and these two houses had been built.

The layout was similar, but my house was definitely more… crowded. I'd lived there for longer than Dex, so that made sense, but he also seemed like he just didn't collect a lot. The walls were pretty bare, but he had furniture, and everything was clean.

"Hey Toby!" Jude said, eyes bright with a half a smile on his face.

"Don't say it," Dex warned me quietly, but Jude only stared at me expectantly. It took me a second, but I remembered him listening to the Beatles as they had driven up. I smiled back and said, "Hey Jude. Don't make it bad."

Both Corbin and Dex groaned at the same time, but Jude laughed happily. "That never gets old," he said, winking at me.

"I assure you, it does," Corbin said, his back to us. He opened a cabinet, took out some plates, and turned to hand them to Jude, who walked over to the table to start setting it.

"Can I help?" I asked, and Corbin handed me the silverware next, then grabbed a roll of paper towels to hand to Dex.

I was totally ready for awkward, but the guys didn't let it get that way. They just sort of carried on and included me in the preparations, joking about music and teasing each other good naturedly. If I had any doubts about their relationship, it was definitely put to ease through the preparations. They interacted just like family, and I didn't sense any underlying sexual tension between them. Not that I doubted them when they'd said they were brothers, but hey, I'd read my fair share of adopted brother romances. (What? Taboo was hot when done well!)

They seemed to switch off who was at the stove, but somehow I never ended up there (thank goodness). By the time we all sat down, there was a spread of bacon, eggs, sausage, rolls, butter, jam, juice, and potatoes. It looked like enough to feed an army, but once the guys started eating, I reassessed that.

They could eat. I guess all those muscles used a lot of calories.

We chatted easily as we all ate, and by the time the food was gone, Jude was finishing a story about Dex trying to ice skate. Everyone at the table was chuckling, and it was just… nice. I figured out that there were five brothers in all—Dex, Corbin, and Jude, obviously, and then Liam, who was apparently a computer genius or something. Atlas was the fifth brother, and they didn't say too much about him, other than that he was a loner. I sensed there was a story there, and I tried not to fill one in with my imagination.

"Do you have any brothers?" Jude asked me.

"No. Only child, and my parents and I… Well, we aren't close. We talk on holidays," I said.

"Yeah, most of us grew up as only children too, but when Wilder adopted us we got a whole mess of brothers out of the deal," Jude said. "I'm obviously the cute one," he added, winking.

Corbin rolled his eyes, Dex growled, and I couldn't help laughing.

"Obviously the troublemaker," I joked, adding, "Dex is the cute one."

Dex grabbed my hand next to his on the table, holding it. He wasn't at all shy about his affection in front of his brothers, and it was really awesome. I'd dated in the past, and sometimes guys didn't like PDA, which I totally understood—it wasn't for everyone. Some guys just weren't touchy-feely in general, but that definitely didn't seem to apply to Dex. He had no problem holding my hand, kissing me, or just generally being affectionate.

I loved it. Not only did I love being touched, but I loved how it showed that he was proud we were together. He'd introduced me to them as his boyfriend, for goodness sake. I was still having a hard time getting over that. It was pretty freaking awesome.

We all cleared the breakfast dishes together, and Dex took a few scraps and left them on the open windowsill, muttering something about not getting shit on, which made everyone laugh. I sensed there was a story there. That and the caw I heard reminded me of the delivery van from that morning.

"Oh, hey, I thought I saw a delivery van coming up my drive this morning. They didn't leave anything?" I asked.

The guys all looked at each other, and Dex seemed to be rumbling in his chest. I just sort of stared, getting a little more nervous as no one answered.

Finally Jude said, "Well, look at the time. Corbin and I are gonna go and check out the house next door!"

Corbin looked at him oddly. "We already did that."

"We're going to do it again," Jude ground out between clenched teeth.

"Why?" Corbin asked, looking confused.

Dex just kept growling, and Jude came over and gave him a pat on the shoulder before sighing at Corbin. "Dex and Toby need some alone time," he said, eyebrows raised.

Corbin raised his eyebrows then, asking, "Are they going to have sex again?"

Oh. My. God.

I knew I turned bright red, Dex growled even louder, and Jude sighed and leaned his head back, probably praying for patience. Corbin just looked even more confused, like he had no idea what he'd said wrong.

Jude finally looked at me. "I'd apologize for him, but Dex is just as bad, and you're stuck with him." He smiled at me then, walked over to Corbin, and grabbed him by his sexy man-bun. Corbin growled at him (must have been a thing in their family), but Jude just dragged him out of the house, and I heard them bickering as the front door slammed.

I smiled after them—I had a bad feeling about the delivery, but they were kind of hysterical—then looked over at Dex, who looked at me possessively. Usually that look was hot, but I didn't think he had good news for me.

"Dex?" I asked.

He came over and wrapped his arms around me, hugging me tight. I could feel his nose pressing into my neck, and he was totally sniffing me, which was weird but also kind of sweet, although I was too nervous to be turned on at the moment.

"We took care of it," Dex mumbled into my neck.

"Ok," I said, hugging him back. I enjoyed the closeness for a moment before I asked, "Took care of what?"

I mean, I probably didn't want to know, but at the same time, I couldn't not know. I'd just make up worst case scenarios in my head. Curiosity and my imagination was what made me a good writer. It also made me an anxious mess sometimes, but we couldn't have everything in life.

Dex growled again, and I guessed that the delivery was something from my stalker. It made sense as to why everyone had gotten all weird when I mentioned it. I was trying not to freak out, because it meant the guy knew where I lived. Unless the guy himself had been the one making the delivery.

If that was the case, had they killed the delivery guy? Although the van would still be here if they had, right?

"What happened to the delivery guy?" I asked.

"He's quitting his job," Dex mumbled.

Ok, so still alive then, and probably not my stalker. "Why is he quitting his job?" I asked. Had they terrified him that much?

"He realized he worked for a bad human," Dex answered.

The phrasing and tone was odd, but I didn't have time to figure that out. "Dex, what was in the delivery?" I asked.

"Flowers," he growled.

Ok. Flowers didn't seem so bad, but… "Were they, like, dead flowers? Or poisonous flowers?" I asked.

Dex gripped me tighter. "They had cameras in them."

Holy. Fucking. Shit.

Goosebumps rose on my arms and I gave a shiver. "Cameras?" I squeaked out.

"And listening devices," Dex added, gripping me even more tightly.

It kind of felt like he was all that was holding me together, and I heard him making soft shushing sounds as he picked me up and carried me over to the couch, settling me on his lap. I was shaking, and I couldn't seem to stop.

It had definitely been my stalker. I mean, I thought that, but knowing it… And he had tried to listen and watch me. I would have taken those flowers into my home. He would have seen and heard… I gave another tremble, and Dex bit down on my neck. The slight sting stopped my spiral of panic and grounded me, although I still felt all kinds of fucked up.

"I'll take care of you," he murmured when his teeth let go.

"He knows where I live," I whispered.

"Yes," Dex answered simply. "I'll protect you."

He held me as my thoughts raced, just letting me process everything. I probably needed to call the police. I needed to tell Amy, too, and see if he had sent anything else. I loved my house, and I always felt safe there, but now… It didn't feel safe anymore.

"It's my home," I muttered, and I knew that probably didn't make any sense to Dex.

"I'll stay with you," Dex answered. "Unless you'd rather stay here."

"Ok," I answered, adding, "I have to work, though."

"That's ok. You can work here, someone can stay with you, or you can be home and we'll keep an eye out. We have cameras and lights outside."

I sighed in relief. Dex would take care of it. We snuggled for a moment longer and I got myself under control, and then something occurred to me.

"Cameras outside?" I asked, pulling back and looking at Dex.

He looked almost… sheepish. He rubbed the back of his neck, answering, "Yeah. The lights are cameras. I didn't want anyone sneaking up on you."

Ok. That was… sort of sweet. Sort of stalkerish, but he was my boyfriend, so that made it ok, right?

"I didn't put any in your house," Dex added, looking proud of himself.

Did that mean he'd thought of it and decided not to? Well, at least he had some boundaries, I supposed. I didn't stop to question what it meant that I didn't think I'd mind so much if Dex was watching me in my house. That was sort of sexy… in theory anyway.

"Don't worry, Toby. We're going to take care of it," Dex added, holding me tightly.

I just relaxed against him, here for the cuddles. I had work to do, and phone calls to make, and I still felt super icky thinking about the stalker apparently knowing where I lived, but Dex was going to take care of me.

I trusted him to do just that.

CHAPTER 18

DEXTER

Toby hadn't seemed to mind when I'd said I'd stay with him, which was good. I didn't think I would be able to stay away. I walked him back to his house and he called Amy, but there hadn't been any more messages from the guy. When he talked about calling the police, I let him know it was already handled.

I knew Jude would be calling Liam, and I'd call him myself to check in. At this point, we didn't need the human authorities involved. We would take care of things.

I got Toby settled in with snacks and his computer, and he talked about his book and where he was in it. Apparently he was coming up to the end, and he needed his hero to be in a dire situation followed by a suitable punishment for the evil vampire villain after all that had been done to the witch character.

"It can't be a quick death, you know?" Toby was saying.

"There's torture, dismemberment, starvation…" I rattled off, thinking of different ways he could drag out this evil vampire's death.

"I mean, torture, obviously, but I feel like I'm running out of ideas," Toby said thoughtfully. "Dismemberment, fingernail removal, and getting shot in the kneecap gets old after a while, you know?" he added.

I grunted. Fingernail removal wasn't as truly horrific as the movies made it out to be. There were really much better method of torture.

"There's always going old school," I threw in.

Toby cocked his head curiously. "Old school?"

"You know, like medieval torture devices. They came up with some truly horrifying stuff. You could have your witch guy thrown in an oubliette to suffer a slow and horrifying death, only of course he gets saved. Then you could have some of the more graphic torture devices used on the evil vampire," I said.

I heard the clacking of Toby's computer. "Oh man," he said, and it sounded equal parts fascinated and freaked out. "Oh, gross, rats," he muttered. I knew I had lost him to research, as he started muttering about iron maidens and pears of anguish.

Ah, the good old days. Although really most of those devices had been used on innocents, but the evil humans who had delighted in their use had a special place in hell reserved just for them.

As Toby got absorbed in his work, I figured he wanted some privacy—that was totally a human thing that they apparently liked—plus, I had a flower shop owner to go torture. I wasn't going to wait until nightfall. I'd rather be back with Toby by then.

"Are you ok here alone? Do you want Corbin or Jude to come over? I have to run some errands," I said.

He paused to look up at me, obviously weighing his decision.

"Unless you'd rather I stay here," I added. Jude or Corbin were perfectly capable of handling the flower shop owner, even if I really did want to do it myself.

"No, I'm ok. Maybe they could just, I don't know, hang out on your front porch and keep an eye out? And let me know if they leave or anything?" he asked.

"Of course," I said. "Someone will always be here." I walked over and kissed him on the head. "I'll think of some torture methods for the bad guy, ok?" I said.

He smiled up at me sweetly. "Thank you," he said, then he was back to his computer, scrolling through a site that had pictures of medieval devices and mumbling to himself.

He was so cute.

With that thought, I let myself out, being sure to lock the door behind me, and headed over to fill Jude and Corbin in and to give Liam a call. There was work to be done, including some fun torture methods to figure out for Toby's book.

It wasn't difficult to track down Kurt, the owner of the flower shop. Finding his address had taken Liam about three seconds. He'd looked into the shop and Kurt's funds, as well, and had noted some abnormally large cash transactions for a flower shop (everyone used credit cards these days). Unfortunately, Toby's stalker hadn't used a credit card, and any records kept online were sketchy at best.

Liam had mentioned coming to the area "to check things out," and as annoying as he could be, I wouldn't mind the extra eyes to watch over Toby.

By the time I got to Kurt's house, it was late afternoon. He lived in a slightly more urban area about twenty minutes from his shop, and his house was large but certainly not a mansion. Luckily, it also had lots of property, so neighbors calling the cops about screaming was not going to be a problem.

Hopefully he didn't have anyone locked up in the basement. I didn't think the oracle would want to adopt another stray human. There were a few other afterlifers in town… But I was getting ahead of myself. No strays would be much better.

As I got out of the car, I took a deep breath in. The stench of a rotten soul was unmistakable.

Unfortunately, so was the smell of smoke and brimstone.

Motherfucker.

I didn't bother with being quiet as I stalked up to the house and in the front door, following my nose to a door that led down steps. Of course they were in the basement, and above the smell of fresh blood, I could smell the coppery undertones of old blood.

I reached the bottom of the stairs and heard whimpering, looking over to see a big guy with short brown hair dangling from a hook in the ceiling. He was naked with a few cuts and bruises, but nothing major. His eyes were pleading with me, but he could only get out muffled whimpers since he was gagged. He got more insistent, shooting his eyes behind me, and I turned around.

"Atlas," I mumbled, folding my arms across my chest. "This was supposed to be my job."

The guy behind me screeched behind the gag, and I heard him thrashing about. I ignored it, staring at Atlas.

He was sitting on a stool against the back wall, wearing jeans and no shirt. He wore a cap over his dark hair and had a scraggly beard, and I wondered how long he had even been in his human form. Atlas preferred his hellhound form. He was… a wee bit feral.

He gestured toward the guy. "I didn't kill him. I just subdued and tenderized him a bit for you."

I sighed, looking back over at the guy. He was in good shape, just a wee bit bruised. I could smell the rot and decay on his soul, a stench he couldn't hide.

"What are you doing here?" I asked without looking away from the human.

"Jude told me about Paradise Falls. I made my way to this part of the country, and when I called earlier, he filled me in," Atlas answered.

Of course he had. Jude was probably the one who kept in touch with Atlas the most, and he wouldn't have known whether Atlas would actually show up, so he wouldn't have thought to tell me.

Ah, well. At least I still got to torture and interrogate the guy. I supposed Atlas had done the messy part of sneaking in and restraining him. I looked around then and noticed that the basement was secure and pretty soundproof.

"Always helps when they have their own torture rooms for us to use," I mused.

The guy whimpered again, and I just rolled my eyes. Evil humans were so badass until they were tied up and bleeding.

I walked over and took the gag out of his mouth, and the guy started blabbering as soon as I did.

"I don't know who you think I am, but I'm not anyone. I haven't done anything, I swear. Please don't hurt me. I don't know what he told you, but I'm not who you think I am," he whined.

"What's your name?" I asked.

"Kurt. I just own a flower shop. I swear. That's all. I'm not involved in drugs or anything," he whimpered.

Ah, so he was involved in drugs too. Made sense. Flowers would be a good way to transport small quantities.

"I'm not here about drugs," I said calmly. "You just need to tell me what I want to know," I said.

Atlas hmph'd behind me. Yeah, yeah, I had implied he'd be ok if he talked. But I hadn't actually said it. It wasn't my fault if the guy was a moron.

"Sure, of course, anything," he whined.

Atlas sighed. "It's so much more fun when you have to break them," he muttered.

"No breaking! I don't need breaking!" the guy shrieked.

I kind of wondered if Atlas had let his hellhound out. The guy was a little too terrified for having a few little cuts and bruises.

"You sent a flower arrangement to Paradise Falls," I said, running my hand gently along his cheek, up to his eye. He closed his eyes as I gently pressed against his eyelid with my thumb.

"Yes! Yes! I did!" he cried out.

"It had listening devices and cameras," I murmured, applying a bit more pressure. Eye gouging was painful, but really it was the psychological aspect that made it most terrifying to humans.

"Yes!" he cried out, then he started blabbering, and I could barely make out what he was saying.

I sighed and took my thumb off his eye, and he blinked rapidly, tears streaming down his cheeks.

"This is boring," Atlas muttered behind me.

I had to agree. Still, I needed information. "Tell me everything," I growled, letting a little hellfire into my eyes.

And he did. It was so easy that it was actually sort of a let down. Apparently he ran drugs, just like I knew from his lie, but mainly in small quantities. His more lucrative side business was catering to stalkers and other creeps. He would send arrangements and gifts with cameras, listening devices, and trackers. He was apparently quite good at his work and very sought after, and he charged top dollar.

As for Toby's stalker—he knew disappointingly little. Yes, he had worked with the guy before. No, he had never met the guy in person. Everything had been done over the phone and through cash deliveries. The guy had watched someone else before this, but the owner couldn't remember his name. He gave me a rough time frame and said it would be in his computer system under deliveries, so I texted the info to Liam to look into. Everything for the listening devices and cameras was online, so he simply gave the guy access to it. I got a password to his computer, and I figured I'd grab that for Liam as well.

"Are you done yet? Is it time for fun?" Atlas asked after it seemed like the guy had spilled all his secrets.

"Doesn't seem like enough for a rotten soul," I murmured.

"Oh, he's done some of his own stalking. You can smell the old blood. I bet he kept someone down here. Probably killed them," Atlas remarked nonchalantly.

"No! I didn't kill her! And it wasn't stalking! We were dating!" he cried out.

I tilted my head. I wasn't so sure about that, despite my actions with watching Toby. Huh. Maybe I shouldn't have placed cameras outside his house? I hadn't microchipped him, though, no matter how tempted I was. Surely that counted for something. And I had told him about the cameras this morning.

"Did she know you were dating?" Atlas asked.

Ah, there we go. That made more sense. This guy was just delusional. Nothing like me and Toby. Toby liked me.

"The bitch thought she could make a fool of me and cheat on me," he spat out.

There it was—the evil creeping out. He ranted a bit more about how he'd been wronged, and women were awful, and they deserved what they got, and blah blah blah.

"Maybe you're actually the problem," I finally commented, then I slipped the gag back up and into his mouth.

"Oh goody, is it time for fun?" Atlas asked.

"Toby needs some ideas for a torture scene he's writing in his book. Something new and interesting. I put him onto medieval torture devices, but none of those are available, sadly. Any suggestions aside from the usual fingernails and cutting and beating?" I said to Atlas.

Atlas hummed as he thought. "There's tooth extraction. Quite painful but not even remotely fatal. We could cut off his dick and shove it down his throat. He seems to have a problem with keeping himself in check when it comes to women. There's flaying—that's pretty old school, and really, it's an art."

The man started crying and screaming behind his gag, but I felt no sympathy. He had tortured women in this very basement. I looked over at Atlas, who pulled a pair of pliers and a knife out of the bag next to him that I hadn't even noticed until now.

"Do I get to help?" he asked.

Brothers. They always wanted to be involved in everything you were doing. I rolled my eyes but motioned him forward. It was nice to see Atlas, after all, and I wouldn't turn down some bonding time.

Chapter 19

Toby

I did a deep dive into medieval torture devices, and it was kind of ingenious for my book. It was also totally something ancient vampires would be into, so it fit my plot perfectly.

Was it weird that I fell a little harder for Dexter every time he gave me plot ideas? I mean, he was totally inspirational for the sex scenes, but he was also really good at helping me talk through my other plot points, and he had great ideas. Not everyone thought talking about torture and dismemberment was fun, but it was totally our love language.

Awww, we had a love language. I was so there for that. Boyfriend goals, activated.

Ok, I knew I was getting corny, but my brain was mush after all the research and writing I'd done. I put my computer down and stood up and stretched. I felt like I'd been working for days, but only a couple of hours had passed. I wondered if Dex was back from his errands? I wondered if it would be weird to go check?

I meandered out onto my front porch and looked over at Dex's house. Corbin was sitting in a chair on the porch, and there were crows lined up on the railing in front of him.

Because, you know, that was totally normal. They all seemed to look my way at the same time, which was also super weird. I gave an awkward little wave, and he gave a head nod in my direction. I debated walking over there, but before I could make a decision Corbin called out, "Dex, Toby is done working."

I heard a muffled sound from inside, then Corbin called over, "He'll be right over!"

I gave my awkward little wave again and headed inside. Ok then. Dex was coming over. And he was… gonna stay the night? Hang out? Have sex with me?

Was it bad that I really hoped we were gonna have sex?

Should I shower? I mean, I'd showered this morning, and then I'd sat on my couch and worked, so it's not like I had worked up a sweat. But, you know, if sexy things were on the horizon…

I ran upstairs to my en-suite bathroom, figuring getting myself ready was better than an unsexy moment. I rushed through some preparation and cleaned myself up. I debated throwing some ball cream on that Sebbie had gotten me as a joke, and I opened the container and took a whiff of the stuff. It definitely smelled strong, but it wasn't a bad smell. I didn't want to smell like I was expecting something, though, and what if Dex noticed the smell?

Yes, that was totally a weird thought, but Dex was always sniffing me, and what if he didn't like the scent of the stuff? I didn't always like the smell of lotions. What if he went to give me head and gagged on the taste of it? It probably tasted awful. Lotion and lube both usually tasted awful. Unless it was flavored lube, I guessed, but I didn't have any of that.

So, definitely no ball cream. And did I even have condoms? I had lube, because, you know, of course I did. But I didn't think I had con-doms. And maybe Dex wasn't even expecting to do anything, and I was getting way ahead of myself.

"Toby?" I heard as my front door slammed.

"Relax, Toby. If he wants to have sex, you're prepared, and if he doesn't, then it's fine," I muttered to myself.

I could hear his steps coming quickly up the stairs, and I opened the bathroom door just as he came into the bedroom.

He was freshly showered, because his hair was still damp and his shirt was clinging to his chest. It looked like he had hopped out of the shower and headed straight here, and my dick perked up at the sight of him. Fuck, he was so sexy.

And who was I kidding, because I definitely wanted to have sex with him.

It totally looked like he sniffed the air, and then he was prowling towards me, because that was definitely the word for how he moved. I had the urge to run, not because I wanted to get away from him, but because it would be hot as fuck for him to catch me.

I backed up toward the bed, and he stripped his shirt off as he got closer.

Yes, please.

When he got to me, he dragged my shirt off, and then his mouth found mine.

God, he was the best kisser. His lips were firm yet soft, and his tongue flirted with mine, his teeth occasionally nibbling. When I bit his lower lip and tugged, he made that super sexy growling sound again, and my dick jerked in my pants. That sound made me so freaking horny. He was turned on, and I was the one turning him on. It was a heady feeling.

He gently pushed me onto the bed, and as I leaned up on my elbows, he grabbed my pants and slid them and my underwear off in one slick pull. Thank god I wasn't wearing socks. I hated only having socks on. It was so unsexy.

Before I got lost down that rabbit hole, he was kneeling in front of me, but I whined low in my throat. Fuck, I wanted him naked, too. I wanted to see that sexy body.

"What, baby," Dex said, reaching out and caressing my very hard cock. I threw my head back and groaned, but I managed to pull myself together enough to look up at him.

"I wanna see you naked, too," I murmured.

He smiled wickedly, and I felt tremors throughout my whole body. He was looking at me like I was the finest steak dinner and he couldn't wait to devour me—it made me feel so unbelievably wanted.

He stripped out of his pants, and he wasn't wearing any underwear (or socks, thank goodness). I barely had time to wonder where his shoes were when my attention was caught by his dick.

Holy.

Shit.

I knew he was big, but seeing it up close and hard and him fully naked? Yeah. Wow. I loved a big dick—although it had been quite a while. I loved a big dildo in the meantime. I loved the feeling of being filled up, and from the looks of it, I had more than I bargained for with Dex.

I couldn't help myself. I slid off the bed down onto my knees in front of him. He looked down at me and gently slid his hand along my scalp, through my hair, giving me goosebumps. I looked up, and what I saw in his eyes made me wanna cry, and I didn't even know why. He looked at me like I was the whole world.

I'd been in love before, and I'd seen guys look at me with love, and I swear that was the intense look Dex was giving me now. But it was too soon for that, wasn't it?

Fuck.

I looked down at his delicious dick again, and his hand tightened on my hair as he growled, and that so did it for me. I grabbed my own dick, just because I needed some fucking pressure, and then I gently kissed along Dex's cock, licking the drop of precum from the tip.

He smelled and tasted like a campfire, which was kind of weird but also hot as fuck. It was all smoky, musky heat, and when he growled again, I took his cock fully in my mouth, being careful to keep my lips over my teeth. He was hard and hot, and I loved having cock in my mouth. Fuck, it was a rush to feel someone come undone while you sucked them.

He gently tugged my hair again, and I moaned in pleasure. I couldn't help stroking myself as I bobbed up and down and licked along his head, using my other hand to gently caress his balls.

"Fuck yeah, baby. Touch yourself for me. You like sucking my cock? It turns you on?" he asked.

Ohmygod, the sexy talk. I was so here for the sexy talk. And the way Dex growled it out? Such a fucking turn on.

I murmured an "Mmmhmmm" around his dick and looked back up at him. I popped off long enough to say, "Use my mouth, Dex."

He growled again, and then he was gently pulling on my hair. I loved the feeling, and he didn't get too rough. It was like he was totally in tune to what I liked. He used his hand to hold me steady as he pumped in and out of my mouth. He was slow at first, and I groaned and tried to move my head faster, only his hand was holding me firmly in place.

Fuck, that was hot. I stroked myself faster, and he fucked into my mouth faster. I could feel him going deeper and deeper, and I wanted to feel full of him. I wanted to take him all. I wanted to gag on his cock and feel him in my throat. I wanted to give him pleasure.

He thrust in deeper, and I pumped my own dick, getting more and more turned on. I felt so fucking sexy knowing I was making him lose control. I groaned—I wanted him all. God, I wanted to feel him all.

It was like he was a fucking mind reader, because he dragged me down his cock, and I felt him in my throat. I relaxed as he murmured above me, "That's it, baby. Yes, that's it. You are so fucking good. You feel so fucking good on my cock."

He was in my throat, and I swallowed around him as he growled steadily. I was pumping myself, and I knew I was going to come the moment he did, but he used my hair to pull me off his cock before either of us got there.

I looked up at him, whining low in my throat. I knew I was probably a slobbery mess, but he looked at me with pure passion. I swear I saw flames licking in his eyes.

"My turn," he rumbled, and he leaned down and picked me up, tossing me on the bed behind me.

Like, literally fucking tossing me. He was so fucking strong, and he was hard and turned on for me.

He was on me before I could even lift myself up onto my elbows, devouring me with his mouth, our cocks rubbing together as we both moaned.

"You want me to fuck you, baby?" he rumbled in my ear when he pulled away from my mouth, and I mewled as he bit down on the tip of my earlobe.

"Yes, Dex. Please. I want you inside. Want you to fill me up," I moaned.

I needed him. Needed him inside me. Needed him all over me. I didn't think I'd ever been so fucking turned on. I made a whimpering sound I barely even recognized, and Dex was sliding down my body, his hot mouth stopping to lick at my nipples.

I was one giant erogenous zone, and my nipples were hard little peaks as Dex laved at them. Before I could get frustrated, he slid down, biting at my hip and causing me to jerk, and then he lifted my legs up and separated my ass cheeks with his hands, and holy fucking fuck he totally bypassed my dick and leaned in to suck on my hole.

He went at me the same way he kissed me—all nibbling and tongue and firm lips, no hesitation, only passion. He was growling against me, and I was whimpering and mewling, unable to help myself. Then he slid something inside me, and I thought it was a finger, only it felt bigger than that, and I didn't even have time to process what the fuck, because it felt otherwordly. It was warm and hard and thick, but not so thick that it hurt as he eased it in, and then he… fuck, he was fucking moving around inside me.

I was panting and couldn't stop, and I thought I was gonna come, because whatever he was doing… I couldn't even explain it. He pressed against my inner walls, and he found my prostate like he had a fuck-ing homing beacon. I cried out as he flicked against that bundle of nerves, sending sparks flying through my whole body. Again and again he thrust into me, sending me flying higher and higher, the pressure building up in my spine. I felt like my whole body was full of electricity.

I almost came, only his hand came up and grabbed the base of my dick. He eased off my prostate, grumbling, "Not yet, baby."

"Please, Dex, please," I cried out. I couldn't take all the pleasure. My entire body was on overload. "I need…" I whined out, and I didn't even get to finish before he was sliding up me, licking and biting his way along my skin until he was at my neck. He used his hands to grab both of mine, pressing them into the mattress. My ass was on a pillow, although I didn't even remember that happening, and his dick teased my hole.

Then he was pressing against my hole, wet and hard and hot, and where the fuck had the lube even come from? His hands were on mine, and I didn't know how he was guiding himself in so easily, and I whined as he entered me.

We were both breathing fast and heavy, and I knew he was trying to give me a moment, but I jerked my hips, trying to take him deeper. He growled into my neck, and then he bit down on the spot between my neck and my shoulder as his cock slid all the way into me.

There was that slight burn I loved, but he had opened me up well, and there was no pain, only pleasure. I was so fucking full. His teeth were on my neck, biting down. His cock was in me, filling me up. He was everywhere, surrounding me, and I jerked my hips as he hit my prostate, white hot pleasure traveling down my spine again.

Dex pumped his hips into me, his teeth still holding onto my neck, and why was that so fucking sexy? He started slow, but then he pounded into me, hitting my prostate on every slide in and out. It was almost too much. Too much sensation cascading around me.

I came with a cry, my whole body jerking and spasming, my hips pumping against him and my channel squeezing around him. He growled louder, bit down harder, and I swear he broke the skin, which only made my pleasure more intense. My cum spurted out between us, my dick rubbing against his abs, prolonging the pleasure.

Then, god, it felt like he was getting bigger inside me, like I was stretching, and he was barely moving, but his dick pressed against my prostate relentlessly. There was a slow drag across that bundle of nerves, and it was too much. Too much sensation, too much pleasure. I was full, more full than I'd ever been before, and I swear I could actually feel his hot cum filling me up. I didn't even give a fuck that we hadn't used a condom, although I should have. There was only pleasure, like he was marking me.

His teeth dug into my neck as he growled, and his cock filled me up, and then I came again… still? I didn't even know. I only knew that the intensity was beyond anything I had ever felt, and I didn't think I would survive. But fuck, what a way to go. It went on and on and on, and I didn't know where I ended and Dex began.

It was just… God, it was too much. I felt like pieces of me were breaking off and floating around, like the world was hazy and smoky as flickering light danced behind my eyelids. I had no idea how much time passed while we both moaned and rode the waves of our orgasms. I had never experienced such prolonged pleasure, and I didn't know if it had been two minutes or twenty, although it felt like we'd been locked together for an eternity.

Eventually, I managed to peel my eyelids open. Dex was still on top of me and still hard inside me, although I didn't feel so crazy full anymore. Dex surrounded me with his heat, although he was careful not to crush me. Our panting breaths filled the quiet room, and his head was buried in my neck.

Only… the flickering light wasn't just behind my eyelids.

What the fuck?

"Dex?" I asked, suddenly unsure. "I think the bed is on fire."

Chapter 20

Dexter

I could taste Toby's blood on my tongue, sharp and coppery. Just a little taste—I hadn't bitten down too hard, but I'd broken the skin.

I hadn't been able to help myself.

I had knotted Toby. I had never knotted a human before, but I hadn't been able to control it. My hellhound had taken over, and I still didn't feel entirely in control. My knot had gone down, but I couldn't seem to make myself roll off of Toby, although I was careful to keep my weight from crushing him.

Because I would never hurt Toby.

Protect, protect, protect. Ours, my hellhound chanted in my mind.

When we had both orgasmed, when his blood had hit my mouth, when my knot had filled him up, it was like a tether had snapped in place between us. I was sure it was my imagination, but I felt like I was tied to him. Like we were linked together.

He was mine.

Mine.

"Dex?" Toby said, and he suddenly smelled… not scared, but not the good, soft, sated smell that he had a moment before. "I think the bed is on fire."

I opened my eyes, and, yes, we were surrounded by blue and red flames.

Fuck. Fuckity fuck fuck.

The flames were mostly licking over our skin, and thank the nine hells that Toby seemed totally unhurt by them, which was something to contemplate later. I concentrated hard, reining myself in, and the flames disappeared like they had never been there.

The sheets were… well, probably ruined. They hadn't totally caught fire, but they were smoky and maybe a little charred.

"Uh," I muttered. Toby seemed to smell a little less stressed than when we'd actually been on fire, but he wasn't smelling all happily content, either.

Oops.

I picked my head up and looked down at him, saying, "I don't see a fire."

Because, you know, I'd put it out.

Toby glanced to the side then back at me, raising one hand to cup my cheek while he stared into my eyes.

I slowly blinked them closed, concentrating on hiding my hellhound, except I could feel my hellhound right at the surface, and when I opened my eyes again, I wasn't quite sure it had worked.

Sex with Toby had been amazing, and I'd definitely let my primal side take over. My demonic tail from my half form had even gotten involved, although I don't think Toby realized exactly what I was doing. But fuck, feeling him squeezing around me, being inside him… it was by far the best sex I had ever had in my life. Then my knot… but he didn't seem to know what had happened there, either.

"Um, Dex?" he said, still cupping my cheek.

"Hmmm?" I asked, trying to hide my head back in his neck, because fuck, he smelled so good. Only his hand was firmly holding my cheek, and I didn't want to force it away.

"Your eyes… they're like… on fire, too?" he sort of asked, and then he let me go so I could bury my head back in his soft, sweet scent.

I sniffed at his skin, giving a little lick, and squeezed him tightly. He gently ran his hands along my back, almost like he was comforting me.

"And, ummm…" Toby started, "well, the sheets are, like, smoldering a bit? So maybe I'm under a lot of stress and I imagined the whole flames covering the bed and your eyes glowing thing, but… yeah, the sheets were definitely on fire."

"Just a little bit," I admitted.

"Just.. a little bit? Dex, I don't think things can be just a little bit on fire," Toby said.

"Sure they can," I grumbled. "And they're out now," I added, rolling over so he was on top of me as I started to pet his back. I wasn't sure if a freak out was coming. He seemed calm for now, but he might've been in a bit of shock.

It's not like I had a lot of experience telling humans what I was. Usually I was killing the ones that knew I was different. Or I was rescuing them, and they were all traumatized and stuff and didn't ask too many questions. This was kind of outside my area of expertise.

"Ok," he said, resting against me and tucking his head into my chest. At least he wasn't struggling or running. That was good, right?

Not that he would run away, would he? Because I couldn't have Toby not with me. That would be bad. Very bad. "If you run away, I'll catch you," I rumbled, gripping him tighter.

Probably not the best thing to say, but Toby was mine.

"My Toby," I growled under my breath, unable to help myself. Hopefully he hadn't heard that.

He snuggled in and started petting my chest, so apparently the catching him comment hadn't freaked him out. That was good. You never knew what humans would get weird about.

I let my arms relax and went back to caressing his back. I was growling a little bit, and he could probably feel it, but I couldn't seem to stop. I was still a little feral, and I knew it probably wasn't the best time to have this conversation. But, yeah, I had set us on fire, so I guessed I had only myself to blame.

Even though it was only a little bit on fire.

Which brought me back to my flame. My flame didn't hurt me or other hellhounds, but it sure as hell burned anyone it touched. I could control it, of course, only I hadn't been in control of it during sex. And Toby was definitely not a hellhound. I would have known immediately if he had been.

Theoretically, it should have burned Toby. Only it hadn't. It had been covering both of us, and he obviously hadn't felt a thing.

The sheets… well, they were another matter. They didn't get most of the flame, since it was on us, but they obviously got a bit. I took one hand and nonchalantly patted a slightly smoldering spot next to us on the sheet. Yeah, these sheets were done.

But… why was Toby immune to hellfire? Was he immune to all hellfire, or just mine? Or was it something I controlled without even knowing it during sex? I had no idea, and I was hesitant to test it. I didn't want to hurt him if it was just a sex thing.

"Dex?" he finally asked after a few moments.

"Hmm?" I answered, kissing his neck, then giving it a little nibble where I had bitten down. He shivered underneath me. Maybe I could distract him…

"No distracting me," he murmured.

Shit.

"It's your fault," I muttered. Which also probably wasn't the best thing to say, considering I felt him get stiff. I hastily added, "I can't control myself with you. You're too fucking sexy, Toby."

He relaxed against me again, smelling more content. I kept running my hand along his back. Maybe I could distract him—if not with sex, then with something else? He didn't seem terribly panicked or anything. Maybe he would chalk it up to stress.

"Would you like me to make you something to eat?" I asked. "I can cook for you," I added.

"Ok," he said, lifting his head and looking into my eyes.

I blinked slowly again. Were my eyes normal? I didn't even know.

Toby started to extricate himself from my grip. I knew I had suggested the whole getting food thing, but really I just wanted to snuggle up with him and hold onto him forever.

That wasn't exactly practical, though, and after a tiny tug of war on his arm I finally let him go and stood up as well. He grabbed sweatpants to put on, and I couldn't help the growl that escaped me. He only looked over, amused, and gave me a wink.

I sighed and put my own pants on, not bothering with a shirt. Then we sort of stood there until he mumbled, "Ok, food," and opened the door and made an after you gesture.

I walked downstairs, and he followed, so that was good. We sort of of… watched each other as we went. I kept looking back to make sure he wasn't going to run for it. He seemed to be watching me intently at the same time, and it was almost like he was blocking my exit in case I decided to run for it, although why he would think I would leave, I don't know.

We got to the kitchen and I started rifling around in the fridge. Toby didn't have much, so I checked the freezer next. There were some frozen burgers that still smelled good over the icy smell. I'd seen bagels on his counter, so they would work for rolls.

"Burgers ok?" I asked.

He nodded, and I started searching his cabinets and drawers for pans and spatulas and stuff. He climbed onto the kitchen island stool and just watched me.

Maybe he wouldn't ask questions. Maybe we could just chalk it up to sex weirdness. Surely humans had odd things happen during sex, right? What was a little flame, after all? And some tail play and a dick that had a knot? Those were probably the type of things that humans just ignored and didn't talk about. That was fine with me. I could definitely do that.

I turned around and smiled, and Toby smiled back. Good. Everything was normal. Perfectly fine. I was totally human and the flames were just… a little misunderstanding. And the tail and the knot weren't even noticeable. Just good sex.

Yup.

By the time the burgers were almost done, Toby was up and grabbing plates, the bagels (we obviously thought alike), and condiments from the fridge. He put it all at the table, and I brought the pan with the burgers over.

He had one bagel on his plate, and the remaining five from the pack on mine. Was six burgers too many? Was that weird?

One didn't seem enough for him, so I slid the burgers onto the bagels and moved a second one over to his plate. He smiled at me.

We could do this. All perfectly normal. Yes, definitely. We had sex and I was feeding him and we wouldn't talk about flames or anything odd like that.

It wasn't until I took my first bite that Toby asked, "Dragon?"

I choked a little bit on my burger before swallowing my bite. "What?" I asked.

"I'm going with dragon shifter," he said, taking a bite of his own burger and staring at me.

"I… What? No… Dragon shifters don't exist," I mumbled, chuckling a little, even though it sounded odd even to me. "I'm just a perfectly normal human. Nothing to see but… you know, humanness. One hundred percent human."

"Uh huh," Toby said. I swear his eyes were twinkling like he was about to laugh. "You do know that insisting you're 'human' is exactly what a non-human would do. Because we don't usually have to defend our 'humanness.'"

"Uh…" I said, then I took a large bite of burger, because then I couldn't say anything else stupid.

"So there's the glowing eyes. I thought I was imagining them, but I really wasn't, and this wasn't the first time. Then there were the flames, which I also didn't imagine, and which definitely burned my sheets," he said, staring intently at me.

"I'll buy you new sheets," I muttered between bites.

Toby waved a hand. "It's fine. I've got lots of sheets. The point is there was fire. And glowing eyes. And then… I think you're really strong. There are dents in my kitchen island. I noticed them the other day. They're a hand space apart, and you were standing there. I think you gripped my kitchen island so tight that you dented the stone."

Fuck. "I'll replace your kitchen island," I added.

"Dex, that isn't the point," he insisted. He continued, "Then there was the… well, I think there was you outside. The glowing eyes were familiar, the growl, the size… I mean, I thought werewolf at first…"

I snorted in reply. A werewolf. As if I were just a werewolf.

"…but then that wouldn't explain the flames. That size didn't seem big enough for a dragon, but maybe dragons aren't house size after all, because how would they hide if they were, right?" he asked.

Then he was staring at me all expectantly and shit.

I took another huge bite of burger and made a mumbling sound with the food in my mouth.

"Oh," he said, looking disappointed, although he didn't smell disappointed. Then he added, "I guess you are just a werewolf then."

"I am most certainly not a werewolf," I insisted. "Werewolves don't even exist. I don't think," I added, because I'd never run across one, but then that didn't mean everything. There might be some things I didn't know. Maybe.

As I was about to open my mouth again to say I didn't even know what, the front door opened.

I should have heard the steps coming over to the house, but admittedly, I'd been distracted. Plus, the fuckers had been quiet.

"Hey, guys!" Jude says as he waltzed into the kitchen. Corbin followed behind, and of course he had a raven on his shoulder. Because that's not at all suspicious.

I gave them both the stink eye and a growl. "I've got this," I muttered.

"Clearly not, wolfman," Jude joked, grabbing a chair at the table and sitting. Corbin leaned against the wall.

"So I can add excellent hearing to the list," Toby mused. Then he suddenly seemed to realize something, because he turned bright red and looked mortified, staring at me in horror.

Fuck.

I guessed I was about to get the freak out I was hoping to avoid, and somehow I thought I could blame Jude and Corbin.

Chapter 21

TOBY

Oh my dear god in heaven, if Dex had great hearing and could hear conversations in my house from his house, then what the fuck had he heard me say?

It was like a slow motion reel in my head of me talking on the phone about him, of Josh and Sebbie and I staring out the window at him… I mean, ok, fine, I'd called him hot and had probably objectified him quite a bit, but I'd also said he was a serial killer, for fuck's sake.

"You're not a serial killer!" I burst out, only… it did not have the expected result. Because rather than everyone looking all reassured and calm, they looked…

Well, Corbin was staring at the ceiling, but yeah—there was nothing up there. Jude had this kid-with-his-hand-caught-in-the-cookie-jar look, and Dex was glaring at Jude and looking all disgruntled. And vaguely guilty.

"You are a serial killer?" I asked, feeling unsure for the first time.

And yeah, probably that was a delayed reaction, but I wrote paranormal romance and mystery. I'd grown up reading about magic and shifters and vampires. So my boyfriend set the bed on fire—literally. He was still the same, sweet Dex who was going to protect me, and suddenly all these things had started falling into place, and I almost felt vindicated. Like I wanted to call up Josh and be like, "Ha! It isn't just my overactive imagination!"

So I figured he was a shifter of some type, only werewolf had gotten a disgruntled snort (I didn't know what they had against werewolves, but they obviously weren't of that magical persuasion). Dragon had seemed like a good guess. I was still kind of betting on that.

But now they'd totally thrown me for a loop with the serial killer thing, because they all looked guilty as hell. If they were dragons…

"Do you eat people? Like, virgin sacrifices? I am not a virgin sacrifice," I declared.

"Oh, we heard," Jude muttered, and that had Dex reaching over and smacking him upside the head.

"Hey!" Jude yelled, rubbing his head.

"Don't talk about my Toby!" Dex growled.

"He thinks we eat people now!" Jude argued back.

"Children, can you both shut the fuck up?" Corbin sighed from against the wall, then he walked over and joined us at the table, muttering, "Why the fuck am I the most level-headed one? I was just coming to see the show."

I was not a "show," but then I figured from Corbin's disappointed sigh aimed at Dex and Jude that he probably meant them. At the moment, he did seem to be the most level headed one. Jude and Dex were busy glaring at each other, and I thought they were both growling now, although it was really quiet.

Corbin's eyes were… also glowing. Ok then.

"Not werewolves. Not dragons, either?" I asked him.

He shook his head no.

"You all kill people?" I asked, because I was still kind of stuck on that.

Dex grabbed my hand at that, pulling me toward him. "But we only kill very bad humans who are hellbound already. It's like… a public service, you know?"

I looked over at Jude, who was nodding enthusiastically. "Yes, very bad people only. Like murderers and rapists and people who have done really bad shit."

I looked back to Corbin, who was just staring at me, probably trying to gauge my reaction.

"What if I freaked out and told you I was going to call the cops. Would you kill me?" I asked Corbin.

Dex growled low in this throat, pulling me in toward him. "No one will ever hurt you, Toby." His grip was tight but not painful, and he was glaring at Jude and Corbin, like they had just threatened me when I was the one who had asked.

"Nah, we don't kill innocents," Jude declared.

"How do you know?" I asked, snuggling up into Dex's side. He really was super warm and cozy. "I mean, how do you know if they're innocent or not?"

"They stink of rotting souls," Dex mumbled disgustedly, and Jude and Corbin just nodded.

Ok then.

And, yeah, I mean, I probably should be freaking out. My boyfriend and his… brothers? Or whatever they were, were clearly paranormal beings who killed people. But hey, only bad people! I had the urge to giggle a little hysterically and barely held it in.

Hellbound, they'd said. Fire. Glowing eyes. Another form. Corbin's weird connection to crows and ravens…

"Demons!" I shouted.

Corbin made a snorting sound, and Dex mumbled, "Nah. They're not evil or anything, but they're supposed to be based in the under-world. Not that you'd know it from all the interlopers in Paradise Falls," he added.

Ok then, not demons. Although they knew of demons, and some lived in town? But that was something to ponder later. If not demons… "Angels?" I asked.

Corbin snorted again, and this time Jude replied, saying, "We are not a bunch of uptight, snotty angels."

"Not all angels are bad," Dex added. "We got a couple here who are ok. The oracle's mate isn't bad."

Okey-dokey then. Angels also apparently resided in Paradise Falls, along with an oracle. And I still wasn't guessing correctly. I felt like it was on the tip of my tongue, like I should really know this. They had fire, they knew angels and demons, they killed bad "hellbound" people, their eyes glowed, and Dex had a habit of growling…

"Hellhounds!" I shouted triumphantly, sure I had gotten it this time.

Dex hugged me tighter, growling in a pleased way, and I looked over to see Jude and Corbin both nodding.

So… my boyfriend was a hellhound.

Ok. I could deal with that.

They were all staring at me now, maybe waiting for panic or something. But panic was not first on my list. I could panic later.

I stood up, disentangling myself from Dex's arms despite his grumbly growling when I did so. I walked over to the kitchen drawer as they all watched, pulled out a notepad and pen, and came back to the table to sit down.

"I have so many questions," I said, starting to jot down what I already knew.

I thought I heard a groan from someone, but I ignored it. They owed me answers, and I suddenly felt like there was a new paranormal series in my future.

By the time Jude and Corbin left, I had pages of notes. I really thought they'd both totally made up the need to go do "moving stuff," but I figured I had interrogated them enough for now.

"So, you guys live for, like, who knows how long, and you used to be based in hell, but ages ago hellhounds came 'topside' and stayed, and they have little hellhound babies that carry on their work," I summed up.

Dex nodded absently. He was at the stove cooking something, and it smelled delicious. He'd found chicken in the freezer and pasta in the pantry, and he was making some kind of creamy, yummy looking sauce to go with it.

"Not a lot of babies, though. My parents only ever had one child. I kind of think hellhounds are born based on the world's population or something, although we never checked that or anything," he commented.

I hadn't asked too many questions about Jude and Corbin's parents—I thought that was kind of intrusive, but Dex had shared his background. As far as he knew his parents were still alive and hunting, although he didn't talk with them regularly. He didn't seem terribly disappointed by that fact, so I tried not to project my own parental insecurities onto him.

I'd gotten the details on demons and angels and oracles—and that last one was apparently Cassius, the coffee shop owner. Who also saw ghosts? So they were real too. And that was kind of creepy, but Dex had assured me I wasn't haunted, and I didn't ask how he knew, because I really didn't want to worry about it.

There was still one question I hadn't asked though, but I didn't know quite how to ask it.

Hey, honey, did you chop off a guy's fingers so I could write my murder scene?

If he didn't, that would be super weird to ask. If he did… Well, really bad people only, right?

How twisted was it that I thought it was even kind of sweet if he went out and did research for me? I mean, that was sort of romantic in a serial killer way, right?

I wondered for a brief moment if I was having some sort of psychotic break. Could this seriously be my life? Never mind that I was taking this all really well. Sure, writing paranormal novels for years had probably prepped me, but still. I was impressed with myself and my total lack of freaking out. Although I supposed deep down I'd known for a while that Dex was different. I'd been only partly joking about him being a serial killer.

Still, I trusted him completely. Maybe that was beyond stupid, but I felt connected to him. I had faith that he would protect me with his life. I knew he wouldn't lie to me. At the risk of sounding super corny, I felt deep in my soul that he was good, despite whatever he might do. And he was mine, and I was his, for however long he'd have me.

Which… yeah, was a problem. I hadn't brought it up, but I was just a regular human. They'd even confirmed that for me when we'd been chatting. Which meant that I had a normal human lifespan, and Dex obviously did not. I would get old and die, and Dex would still be around. For a really long time, by the sound of it.

It made me sad to think of him all alone. Not that he'd be totally alone, because he had his brothers, but still. When I'd casually asked them about previous relationships, they all sort of looked at me blankly, like the idea of being in a relationship was totally foreign to them. So obviously they didn't normally date humans.

I didn't know what that meant for Dex and me, but I figured we had time to figure it out, and one worry at a time was enough.

Dex brought dinner over to the table, and it tasted as delicious as it looked. After we'd both had a few bites, I asked, "Were you, um, working earlier?"

"Yes. I called Liam and filled him in before I came over. We got the guy who planted the listening devices, but he had very little info on your stalker. He stalked someone in the past, although we don't have a name, but Liam is trying to track down who it is. In the meantime, we'll never leave you alone. And we'll smell if a rotting soul is in the vicinity," Dex assured me.

I had my very own supernatural protection team. It was comforting.

"If you need some help with that scene, I also have some ideas for you," Dex added nonchalantly.

Ok then, I guess that answered that question. Maybe I should be disturbed, but, well, I was a writer; we got inspiration wherever we could. Yup, that was my story, and I was sticking to it. Plus, only really bad people.

I filled him in on my current plotline while we ate, and he added ideas and answered questions. He had some unique new torture methods I could throw in for the evil vampire, although he made sure to not get too gruesome, and he did grudgingly add that his brother Atlas had shown up and had "told him" quite a few of the ideas.

We were in the middle of talking about flaying (kind of gross, and who knew someone could live so long through that process?) when my phone started ringing.

I checked it, saying, "It's Josh," for Dex's benefit.

"Go ahead. I'll clear the dishes," he replied, grabbing the plates from the table.

"But you cooked. I'll clear," I said as I picked up the phone, saying, "Hey Josh."

Dex just winked at me and carried on clearing the table.

"Hey," Josh answered.

"My neighbor is a hellhound," I gleefully proclaimed. Dex just stopped what he was doing to stare at me.

"That's nice," Josh said. "Thinking of a new series?"

Dex was staring at the phone, and I figured he could probably hear Josh's side of the conversation as well. They had great hearing, apparently.

"Yup!" I said. "They kill people, but only really bad people," I added.

"That's cool. I think that'll be popular. Bad guys who aren't really bad. Everyone loves a morally gray main character," Josh replied.

"Yeah. And they're super sexy with muscles and glowing eyes and all the growling," I sighed, because Dex was super sexy. "Oh, and Dex is my boyfriend," I added.

"Oh my god, Toby! Seriously! That's awesome! Congrats! Give me all the details!" Josh gushed.

I chuckled, "I totally will, but how are you? All ok? You still sound a little… tired," I said carefully.

"Problems with Rick," Josh sighed. "I think it might be time to call it quits, but it's hard. We've been together awhile, but things just… they haven't been good. At all." He paused, but then he forced a cheery voice and said, "But I don't want to talk about that right now. I called you for a cheer up, so fill me on your new boyfriend, and spare no details."

So I filled him in, although I did spare a few details. At one point, Dex's phone rang as well, and he went out onto the porch to take it, but I knew he wasn't far.

I was safe. I was protected. I was dating a hellhound. And, if I was being honest with myself, I was probably in love with him as well.

But that bombshell could wait for another day. I think today had been eventful enough.

Chapter 22

Dexter

I have to admit a moment of… well, not panic, because I was a hellhound, and I did not panic. But it had definitely taken me by surprise when Toby had just up and told Josh what I was. Of course, Josh didn't believe him, and I expected that Toby knew that would be the case.

Toby did have an overactive imagination, but I was still aggravated on his behalf. He wasn't lying. I was a hellhound, and his best friend didn't even believe him. Maybe I'd go all glowy eyes on Josh next time he was around. I chuckled to myself a little. I knew it shouldn't be funny to think about startling Toby's human friends, but, well, they really ought to believe him.

My phone rang while Toby was on his, and I stepped outside to take it since it was Liam. He started without even a hello.

"No luck on tracing the emails, which I didn't expect, but after some careful combing through records I found the guy that was probably stalked before Toby. He had a delivery around the date your guy mentioned, and he filed a police report about a stalker before that. There were emails, phone calls, and complaints of being followed," Liam said, keys clicking in the background.

"Wait—are you saying we have a name?" I asked, feeling gleeful.

"Well, sort of," Liam hedged.

I growled.

"So the guy was a bartender in an upscale restaurant, and he had some guesses as to which customers he found 'creepy' and who he thought it might be, but he gave the cops a couple of names," Liam said.

"Ok, well that's better than nothing. You can start looking into them," I said.

"Already done. Here's where things get… tricky. Our bartender disappeared. He hasn't turned up again. No credit cards used. No funds accessed. No social media posts," Liam said.

"Dead?" I asked.

"Probably," Liam admitted. "That was over a year ago. Police questioned everyone he had given names for, but they all had alibis, and there was no body and no sign of foul play. No sign of struggle in the guy's apartment, either. His phone, computer, wallet, and a suitcase were gone as well, so it couldn't be proven that he hadn't just up and left. The police couldn't very well press charges against anyone with no proof of anything."

"Fuck," I said. "So what about the suspicious guys? And where was this?" I asked.

"About two hours north of you. So I've got three names, and I started looking into them," Liam said.

"We can go and check them out. I can send Jude and Corbin while I stay with Toby. If this guy stalked and kidnapped someone, they'll be able to smell his rotten soul a mile away," I said.

"Good. I'm going to wrap up some things here and then head to Paradise Falls as well," Liam said.

I groaned. "Coming to the rescue," I joked.

"Hey, if we're buying that property, which apparently we are since Jude's bid for the house was accepted, then I want to check it out," Liam admitted.

Huh, I hadn't realized they'd already finalized buying the house next door. Plus, more eyes on Toby wouldn't be a bad thing.

"Oh, Atlas is around, too," I added.

I heard a pause in the clicking. "Is he?" Liam asked.

"Yeah. He talked to Jude and was at the flower shop owner's house. I forgot to tell you. He didn't come back with me, but I didn't really expect him to," I added.

"Yeah. The place must have his seal of approval, though, or he would have let us know. I'm sure he'll pop up at some point," Liam said, starting to type again.

Atlas was… well, he was a loner. He was pack, but he was pretty feral, and we all loved him, but we gave him plenty of space. None of us really won any awards in the growing up department, but Atlas had a really fucked up past. At least we all knew who our parents were, even if they'd died or abandoned us or given us to Wilder because it was for the best.

"Yup," I answered. "Send me the names."

"Done. Keep me posted," he said, and then he was gone.

I heard Toby still chatting on the phone, and Jude and Corbin must have heard most of my conversation with Liam, because they came out of my house and headed over to Toby's porch.

"We heard there are leads," Jude said. "You want us to head out now?"

It was nearing dusk—quite a bit of the day had passed with Toby asking questions—but I was too impatient to wait until morning. Not that it mattered—we were hellhounds. Darkness was natural to us.

"Yeah. I can text you…" I started, but Jude held up his phone.

"Liam already forwarded the info to us. We should be able to track these guys down pretty easily," Jude answered. "I doubt it'll take more than a night."

"Don't worry—we'll hold onto him for you," Corbin smirked.

I nodded, and they walked over towards their car.

It felt… anticlimactic. Not that I wanted Toby kidnapped, but I couldn't seem to shake that dream I'd had. There was no way, however, that anything would happen to him with me here, and chances were good that Jude and Liam would track the guy down. Not only that, but even if someone did take Toby, I would be able to find him. His scent was permanently engraved in my nose, and his taste was in my mouth. I felt tied to him, and I knew I could hunt him down anywhere.

It was comforting.

Not sure if Toby would see it that way, but he didn't have to know about it.

I listened to him talk to Josh from the front porch, and eventually their conversation wound down. When he got off the phone, I headed back inside, filling him in on my conversation with Liam.

He looked a little nervous hearing about his stalker, and I swooped in to give him a kiss, ready to take his mind off that unpleasantness. Before it could get too heated, he put a hand on my chest.

"I just realized… I mean, I realized before, but…" he hesitated, biting his lip. It was so cute, but he smelled unsure, and I didn't want that.

"What is it, baby?" I asked.

"They can hear us," he whispered in my ear.

I looked at him, perplexed. "Who can hear us? I got rid of the listening devices and the camera."

Toby rolled his eyes at me. "Your brothers, you goof. They can hear us"—he leaned in then, whispering—"having sex."

Ahhh. Yes, humans were shy about things like that. Still, I leaned back and let my eyes twinkle.

"Why, Toby, did you have something in mind for our evening?" I joked. "Maybe you'll just have to be very, very quiet."

He laughed. "Yeah, good luck with that. I can't help myself with you."

I smiled, grabbing his hand and attempting to pull him upstairs. I didn't think he was ready for another full round—he had taken my knot, after all, and I wouldn't hurt him—but we could get up to a little fun.

He pulled against my hand, though, stopping me. I could've easily dragged him along, but I didn't want Toby uncomfortable. "They went out," I told him. "No one is around to hear."

"What about if one of your other brothers gets here? Liam or Atlas? You told me that you ran into Atlas, and Liam said he's coming. How far away is he?" Toby asked.

I had no idea what the answer was to either of those questions.

"Huh," I said, stumped.

Still, this would not do. My brothers were moving in next door, for fuck's sake. They were currently staying in my house. I would not be permanently cock blocked because hellhounds had good hearing.

"What about, like, background sound?" Toby asked.

One of the things I enjoyed about living next to Toby was that he didn't always have a radio or tv blaring. He liked the quiet, and it was peaceful, but if that made him more comfortable…

"Yeah, if you put on some background noise it will cover up our noise," I said. I didn't add that it would also be a dead giveaway that we were having sex. If it made Toby feel less self-conscious, that was fine by me. I'd have to remember to tell the pack not to mention sex because humans were weird about it.

Toby went over and fiddled with a bluetooth speaker and his ipad, eventually putting on a playlist. He turned the volume up quite high as well. I probably grimaced, because he pulled me along up the stairs and into his bathroom, where the sound was at least somewhat muted.

I didn't know what Toby had in mind, but I was totally on board for a shower together. I started stripping my clothes, and when he just watched, I finished and started stripping him. We were under the hot spray in a few moments, and he thoroughly enjoyed soaping up my body, murmuring about my muscles and tattoos the whole time.

If I flexed a little for him, who could blame me? It was beautiful to be admired by Toby. I could only take so much, though, before I growled, "My turn."

He looked self conscious for a moment, but he was perfect in every way. By the time I was done licking, nibbling, and caressing every inch of skin, he just looked like he was floating.

"Dex," he moaned, and I couldn't tease either of us anymore. I pushed him against the wall and took both our cocks in my hand, every slide of his dick against mine pure bliss.

I leaned into him, kissing him, and when the pleasure was too much, we came together under the hot spray, mouths joined, breathing the same air.

I could tell Toby was wiped out, and I helped him out of the shower, drying him off first before I dried myself off. He went into the bedroom and started looking around for clothes, but I dragged him into bed, laying him on top of me and nuzzling into his neck. He smelled so good. I couldn't get enough of his scent, and the place where I'd bitten him smelled like the two of us together.

I caressed him softly until his breathing evened out. I held him close, burying my nose in his skin and eventually fading into sleep myself.

Wrong, wrong, wrong, my hellhound growled in my mind.

I came awake with a start, rolling Toby off of me and behind me in one swift move. It took only a second to know what was wrong.

The stench of rot was in the air.

I had been so ensconced in Toby's scent that I hadn't noticed it right away, but now that I was out from under him, it was unmistakable.

And it was close.

The damn music was still playing, and if a car had approached or there was someone in the house, I'm not sure I would have heard them.

"Dex?" Toby whispered behind me, his voice sleepy and confused.

"He's here," I growled.

"Fuck, fuck, fuck," Toby whispered, sounding wide awake and panicked at my words. "I'll call 911…" he started, but I cut him off.

"No. No human police," I said, grabbing my phone off the nightstand.

"Oh my god, Dex. He's here? Are you sure?" Toby whispered.

I grabbed his hand with mine, using my other hand to open my phone. There were a string of texts from Jude and Corbin, but I didn't bother reading them. I just texted He's here and put the phone down.

I could hear Toby's heartbeat, his breathing fast and shallow, and I could scent the panic on him. I turned to him, keeping an ear on the door. I'd hear even over the music if anyone tried to open it. I would deal with Toby's stalker, but first I needed to calm down Toby.

"Listen to me, Toby. Everything is going to be ok. I will protect you no matter what, ok?" I assured him, using the hand not holding his to caress his cheek.

His grip on me tightened. "What about you?" he asked. "This guy could be dangerous."

"I'm not human. No one is more dangerous than me, Toby," I rumbled. I knew my eyes were on fire, and tiny blue and red flames danced up my arm before I got control of myself. Weirdly, that seemed to reassure Toby. He took a deep breath, nodding his head.

"I'm going with you," he said.

I started to shake my head no, but then I thought about it. Would it be safe to leave him here? I only smelled one rotting soul. Still, I was unsettled that he had gotten this close without me being aware.

"Listen," Toby cut in, "I write suspense. You never separate. You never leave the MC who is being stalked alone. The villain will trick you and grab me somehow. I'm coming with you so I don't get kidnapped."

"If he took you, I would find you. I would hunt you down to the ends of the earth, Toby. I would leave the mortal plane and follow you into the afterlife if I needed to. I will always find you. You are mine," I declared.

Toby looked into my eyes, then he gave me a quick kiss. "You say the sweetest shit. But I'm still coming with you."

I growled, but I got up and threw on some sweatpants, listening for sounds from the house. Toby did the same, trying to keep quiet.

I didn't hear anything other than the music and our own movements. I would almost think I was mistaken, but the stench of rotten soul was overpowering. And it was close.

I opened the bedroom door slowly and quietly, keeping Toby firmly behind me. I listened again, sniffing the air. The music was a distraction, but at this point, I didn't know that turning it off wouldn't give us away to the human.

He was just being so utterly quiet. He must have been lying in wait for Toby. I would have to scent him out, because he wasn't moving.

That was fine. Hellhounds enjoyed the hunt. I just wished Toby had stayed behind. I understood his concern, but I worried about him getting hurt. Underneath that, I had to admit there was also the fear of him seeing me harm another human. Knowing it and seeing it were two different things. I never wanted Toby to be afraid of me.

We crept down the stairs, Toby staying behind me, and I realized that the hellbound soul wasn't in the house. He was outside in the front. I still didn't know if he had driven here and I had somehow missed the sound of the car or if he had parked further away and walked, but the scent was definitely coming from that direction. Perhaps he was just watching the house?

If I didn't have Toby with me, I would go out the back and sneak around to him, but I didn't want to draw this out. Toby was nervous, and I wanted the human subdued.

"Wait here," I whispered, and before Toby could protest, I threw open the door and rushed out the front steps.

I saw the gun the moment I was clear of the door, and I had only a fraction of a second to make a decision. If I dodged the bullet, it could hit Toby, and he was only human.

I couldn't chance it.

"Run!" I cried out to Toby, then I heard the gunshot and there was darkness.

CHAPTER 23

Oh my god, oh my god. He'd shot Dexter. He'd shot Dexter in the fucking head and there was blood and Dexter was down and I could see a figure slowly walking toward the house in the darkness.

Dexter had told me to run; that had been the last thing he said.

I didn't know if he was alive or not. Dear god, please let him be alive. I couldn't lose him. I couldn't. He meant too much to me. I'd just found him. He had to be ok.

I'd watched him get shot in the head. No one could survive that.

But he was a hellhound. They lived a long time. They were strong. They were "practically invincible," they'd said, when I'd been asking questions.

I wished I'd asked what the "practically" part meant.

I wanted to check on him, but I knew there was nothing I could do, and I knew if he wasn't dead, the guy would probably finish him off if given the opportunity. I did the only thing I could think of to get him away from Dex; I did exactly what Dex told me to do.

I ran.

I didn't bother shutting the door—I wanted him to follow me and not stop at Dex. I ran through the house and out the back door, flinging it open and careening down the back steps. I could hear footsteps behind me, and I headed straight out into the forest. Maybe I could lose him. Maybe I could distract him enough for Jude and Corbin to get here, and they could do something, and Dex would be ok.

Dex had to be ok.

There was no point if he wasn't. If he was dead… But he couldn't be. I felt like he was still with me, like he was still a piece of me. I pressed my hand to the mark on my neck where he had bitten me, and I… I could do this. I would do this. Dex would want me to stay safe, and I would do what Dex wanted.

His brothers would come, and they would fix him. That was all there was to it, and I refused to let myself think anything else.

I ran, dodging trees and stumbling over branches. I knew I was being too loud and my breath was coming in great gasps. Convincing myself that Dex was ok pushed some of the panic back, and I slowed down, trying to quiet myself.

Someone was following behind, crashing through the underbrush just as loudly as I had been, but I could hear them slowing down now that I wasn't blundering through the woods.

I put my hand over my own mouth, trying to calm my breath, and started quietly darting from tree to tree. It was dark as hell out, and I knew if I couldn't see him, he couldn't see me, either. I just needed to stay away from him. Maybe I could backtrack to the house without him knowing? I would try. I knew these woods better than him. I'd walked through them plenty of times while thinking and plotting.

I almost laughed at that. I was in my own fucking suspense novel.

"Toby?" a voice called out. "Toby? Where are you? We're here to help. Toby!" the voice yelled out.

Bullshit. I wasn't stupid.

"We got a call from your neighbor about a gunshot, and we found someone dead on your porch," the voice said.

Lies. Lies. Lies.

"Toby, the neighbor said they saw someone else. We know it wasn't you who shot the guy. We're looking for the perpetrator now. We need to get you to safety, though," the voice called.

I kept creeping along. I wasn't a fucking idiot. If it were the police or first responders or whoever, they would have identified themselves first, and there would have been more than one voice.

I quietly continued to creep along. I needed to double back to check on Dex, but I didn't want to run into the stalker. I sort of knew where he was based on his voice, but it was hard to pinpoint sound in the woods. I just knew it was behind me. Still, I couldn't let him push me further and further away from civilization.

I started heading sideways, towards Dex's and Patricia's houses. I didn't want to involve Patricia, but if I could get into Dex's house, I could call the cops. I knew Dex had said no human police, but I think we were a little past that.

"Toooo-beeeeey," a voice called out, and it sent shivers down my spine.

The man laughed. "Of course you wouldn't fall for that. You're too smart for that. I know that. It was why I was so attracted to you to begin with."

Yes, just keep talking. I quietly crept along, going sideways instead of further back into the woods, trying to avoid the voice in the darkness.

"You don't know me, I know that, but I have only your best interests in mind. I know exactly what you need, Toby. I've read all your work, more than once. I know what you cry out for. The protection and the undying love—I can give that to you, Toby," he said.

I stumbled on a branch, a cracking noise interrupting the silence. Shit! I quietly moved as fast as I could to get away from where I had made the noise, but when his voice started again, it was closer.

"I'll give you everything you ever desired. I know your deepest fantasies, and I can make them all come true, Toby. You just have to trust me," he called out.

Fuck. He'd figured out which way I was headed. I crept quickly and quietly, trying to backtrack now. Fuck it. I would hopefully get back to one of the houses first. I wasn't even sure if I was behind mine or Dex's, but it didn't matter.

"I know it wasn't you who blocked me. I know it was that bitch of a PA. Don't worry, Toby, she's been taken care of," he called out.

He had to be lying. I'd talked to Amy this morning, and she was a plane ride away from here. There was no way he had gotten to her. He was just trying to draw me out.

I could see lights in the distance ahead now, and I knew that at least I was headed back towards the houses. But if I could see the lights, then there was also the possibility that he'd be able to see me once I got closer to them. Darkness was my friend out here.

I didn't think he'd shoot me, but what did I know? He'd shot Dex in the head—but he was fine; he had to be fine—but that implied he was a pretty good shot. He could probably shoot me in the leg or something, and then I'd be fucking caught.

I didn't know what to do. Shit, shit, shit.

And then I thought I heard it… a low growling sound.

Oh god, please, please let it be a hellhound. Please let it be Dex or Corbin or Jude or fucking anyone.

Then I saw them off in the distance—the little red and blue flames dancing along the back of a tall, dark, hound-like figure. Only it wasn't coming from the direction of the house; it was coming from back in the woods.

It wasn't Dex, but it was a hellhound. Was it Corbin or Jude? I had no idea, but I thought they'd come from a car if they were going to get here. But what did I know? How fast could hellhounds run? I wished I had asked even more questions.

I did the only thing I could think of—I ran towards him. At this point a strange hellhound was far better than my stalker. I had to believe it was someone Dex knew, and Dex needed help.

I didn't try to keep quiet now; I just ran.

"Toby!" the man's voice cried out, and I heard footsteps crashing through the woods behind me, but I didn't care at this point.

"He shot Dexter!" I called out into the darkness, aiming for the hellhound, running as fast as I could. He had stopped and stood still, as if surprised I was running toward him, but at my words he charged forward.

Oh god, oh god, oh god. He was fucking huge, and he was on fire, and his eyes were glowing red, and he was growling, and it was fucking scary. It was not Dexter, and I didn't think it was Jude or Corbin either although I had no fucking clue why I thought that.

The hellhound was careening toward me, and the stalker was running behind me, and I was literally caught between a psychopath with a gun and a creature from hell. I felt like the hellhound was literally going to collide with me, but the stalker was right fucking behind me now. I could practically feel him reaching out to me.

"Gotcha!" he cried out, snagging the back of my shirt. I went down, stumbling over my feet, and I felt the stalker go down on top of me, knocking the wind out of me.

I gasped, trying to catch my breath, feeling the heavy weight on top of me, and then it was gone, knocked off me.

I rolled over and turned around, and there was the hellhound, dripping fire, snarling, and growling. He was standing over the man, who was laying dazed in the dirt. I could see the stalker now in the glow from the flames, and he looked like an attractive and fit guy, which somehow made me even more pissed off. Shouldn't he have some tragic backstory to explain his stalking?

"What the fuck?" he whispered, and then he raised his hand with the gun in it, but the hellhound was too fast for him, snapping his jaw down on the man's wrist.

The man screamed in agony, dropping the gun, rolling around and grabbing his wrist. The hellhound just stood there over him, growling but doing nothing else, and I couldn't figure out why. I wanted to shout at him to finish the man off, even if that was terribly brutal. I wanted him to go help Dex. I opened my mouth to demand that of him, and that's when I saw a figure stalking toward us in the darkness.

Dexter.

He was alive.

Dear god, he was alive, and he was fucking beautiful, flames dancing along his skin as he prowled through the woods toward us. His bare feet and bare chest shone in the moonlight and the glow of his flames, and the dark sweatpants he had pulled on somehow didn't burn away. There was blood on his head and in his hair, trailing down his chest, but he was walking towards us; he was alive.

"Dex!" I sobbed, relief and fear crashing into me, making me shake. I couldn't even get up. I wanted to run to him but I couldn't seem to make my arms and legs work.

He growled as he stared at me, looking me up and down, but I wasn't afraid. I could never be afraid of him.

"I'm ok," I called out. "I thought you were…"

I couldn't even finish it.

He was suddenly in front of me, and it was like it had taken him years and merely seconds to get to me. I knew I was probably in shock or dealing with an adrenaline rush or something; I felt weak and shaky and cold and a little out of it, and I couldn't hold back a sob when I felt his hands close over my arms.

He grabbed me to him, pulling me in close, and his flames licked along my skin, but they didn't hurt at all. He was growling steadily, holding me tightly, and his warmth felt so good against my skin. My teeth were suddenly chattering, and I could only huddle into him.

He was safe. He was alive. He was ok.

"You're ok," I whispered, and he nodded his head against me, still growling. He held me for… I don't know how long. Time seemed funny to me, and it could have been five minutes or an hour. At some point it was like reality came rushing back in, and I realized the man was sobbing quietly behind us. I tried to pull back to look, but Dex only held me tighter.

"Kill him," Dex murmured above me.

There was a growl in response, and the man just continued his low sobbing noises.

"Why the fuck not?" Dex asked.

Another growl, and I had no idea if Dex understood what the other hellhound was saying or not, but he just gave a sigh.

"Toby, this is Atlas. Atlas, this is Toby," he murmured.

I peeked out from behind Dex, and this time he let his hold loosen enough that I could. Atlas was still standing over the man, who was gripping his wrist and writhing in pain, whimpering and crying. There was blood on him, and I tried not to notice that.

"Hi," I said. "Nice to meet you!" And then I giggled a little, because, yeah, this was kind of crazy.

Atlas sort of nodded his head in apparent greeting, then the man rolled a little to the side, and he was right back to growling and snarling at the guy, who went right back to whimpering.

Dex picked me up like I weighed absolutely nothing and started walking back towards the house with me. "Take him to the basement, Atlas," he called over his shoulder.

I snuggled into his chest, and I could smell the smoky, campfire smell that was pure Dex. I closed my eyes, soaking in the warmth and letting everything else but the feel and smell of Dex slip away.

CHAPTER 24

DEXTER

Getting shot in the head was not pleasant.

I wanted the fucker dead. He'd terrorized my Toby. I could still smell the fear on him—an acrid and bitter scent that he hadn't entirely shaken off.

Hellhounds didn't die easily. I'd never known one who'd actually been killed, so I wasn't sure it was even possible. Some things took a little recovery time, though, and getting shot in the brain was something that took a few moments to get over. Hellhounds had the speed to dodge a head shot, but there had been Toby to consider, and taking the shot had seemed the best course of action.

Any other bullet wounds wouldn't have slowed me down, but a head shot required a bit more work. By the time I'd expelled the bullet from my brain and had full awareness back, I'd smelled Toby's fear, the stench of the rotting soul, and, thankfully, another hellhound.

Atlas must have been close by, and Jude or Corbin must've texted him to get over here. Why he wouldn't kill the fucker I didn't know, and he clearly didn't feel like shifting to explain. Maybe he just didn't want to scare Toby; I didn't know if he knew that Toby even knew about us.

So much to figure out, but first, my Toby. He was cradled in my arms, and his shaking had subsided. I carried him into his house and upstairs to his bedroom, pausing only to shut the music off downstairs, which I managed to do without putting Toby down.

I walked into the bathroom, and that's where the dilemma was. I didn't really want to let him go, but I needed to wash off the blood, and Toby was messy with dirt and leaves from the forest.

I managed to grip him with one arm and free a hand to turn the water on. The sound seemed to rouse Toby, because he started to shift like he wanted down out of my arms. I growled but let him stand, making sure he was steady. He stayed huddled into my arms, and I stripped off his shirt, making sure to stay close and keep body contact with him. I managed to slide down my pants and kick them off, and then I slid his off as well, his hands using my shoulders for support when I knelt down.

He still looked dazed and a bit out of it, and I picked him up and carried him into the shower, letting the hot water spray down onto him, making sure his face stayed clear. He eventually seemed to rouse, and he put his hands on my shoulders and made motions as if to get out of my arms.

"I can stand up," he murmured.

I could only growl in response. Maybe it was a delayed response on my part, but it was starting to hit me that Toby had almost been hurt. What if the guy had shot him? What if in the moments the bullet had been expelling from my brain, he'd hurt my Toby? I growled again.

Toby patted my chest. "I'm ok," he murmured, almost as if he could sense my thoughts. "I'm ok, and you're ok, and the guy is in the basement or whatever."

I let his legs slide down from my arms, making sure to support him in case he was still shaky. He held onto my shoulders, and he seemed steady enough. He looked up at me, and I saw tears in his eyes. He reached up and touched my head, and I realized the blood was still there.

I ducked my head under the water to rinse it away, saying, "It takes a lot more than bullets to kill me."

"What does it take?" he whispered. "I thought… Fuck, Dex."

"I don't even know that we can die. I've never known a hellhound to die. So you don't need to worry about that, ok, baby?" I reassured him.

"Let's get you clean."

I gently soaped him up, washing his body and his hair. When I was done, he did the same for me. We both ended up slightly turned on, but we both knew that wasn't what we needed.

I would make Toby mine later and claim him in that way, but right now, I just needed to care for him. He apparently felt the same way, because his soft hands lightly caressing my skin were almost reverent.

We were both ok. We needed to just feel each other to make sure of that.

When we were done, I shut the shower off and dried us off. He stayed huddled into me, which made it slightly difficult, but I wanted him to stay exactly where he was—pressed against me.

When we were dry enough, I carried him into the bedroom and lay on the bed with him, wrapping him in my arms and nuzzling into his neck. Our hands traced over each other's bodies, and we just touched and lay together, breathing and calming down.

I don't know how much time passed, but eventually I heard the sound of a car coming towards the house. I almost tensed, but I could hear the music as well, and I knew it was Jude and Corbin. No one else would be blasting The Beatles coming up the driveway.

The music shut off, and I heard two car doors slam.

"Dex," I heard Jude call out.

I sighed, and Toby lifted his head to look at me.

"Are you ok?" I asked him.

"Are your brothers here?" he asked. He must have heard the car doors as well.

"Yeah," I answered.

"You need to go talk to them and find out what's going on," Toby told me. "It isn't really over. That guy is in your basement. And I don't wanna know what you do to him, but I wanna know when he's taken care of. And I need to call Amy to know that she's safe, too."

"Can Jude and Corbin sit with you? I don't want you alone," I commented, kissing his forehead. I smelled a pleased, happy smell from him, and it was a welcome scent after his fear.

"Yeah. But maybe we can get dressed and meet them downstairs?" Toby suggested.

"Yes. And you need to eat," I added. Humans could go into shock, and I should've fed Toby and gotten him some hydration before now.

"Yeah. I'm ok, but I do still feel shaky from the adrenaline, and you're right that some food will help," he agreed.

We got up and dressed, heading downstairs to meet Corbin and Jude. They had let themselves in, and Corbin was already at the stove cooking. Jude was out on the front porch, waiting to talk to me, I was sure.

I pulled Toby in for a hug and gave him another kiss on the forehead.

"I love you, Dex," he said, hugging me tightly.

I felt like my heart was going to beat out of my chest. I had never had anyone tell me that before. I had never said it, either, but somehow the words flowed easily off my tongue. "I love you too, Toby. More than life itself."

He smiled and nodded against me, then he gave my butt a playful swat and pulled away, putting on a smile as he turned to face Corbin. "Thank god you're cooking, because I suck at it," he joked.

Corbin looked over and smiled, and a crow flew down from who knew where and left a shiny, smooth pebble on the kitchen island in front of Toby, hopping back and forth on the island. Toby looked enchanted by the gift, and he sat down, watching the crow.

"I get shit on, and he gets pretty pebbles," I muttered.

Toby laughed, and I walked over to kiss him again before I headed toward the front door. "I'll be right next door. You just yell if you need me," I said, and Toby nodded and smiled at me.

I turned and walked away, and I had to fight down my flames. Just thinking about that fucker…

"Whoa there, killer," Jude joked when I got to the front porch. He talked quietly enough that Toby wouldn't be able to hear us.

"Is he dead?" I ground out.

"He's in the basement with Atlas. He was waiting on you," Jude commented. "Did you check your texts?" he asked.

"No. We were sleeping, then he shot me in the head," I added.

"Too slow to duck, old man?" Jude joked.

"I was afraid the bullet would hit Toby," I answered, and Jude sobered instantly at that.

"Yeah, well, one of the guys was evil but not our guy, and Corbin took care of him while I checked out the others. The second guy was an innocent, so I left him alone, and the third guy was in the wind, which was what I texted to let you know. I'm assuming that's our guy who is currently being held downstairs."

I nodded once. I didn't understand why we even needed to talk about this.

"Dex, this guy stalked someone else a year ago according to Liam," Jude stated.

"Yeah, Liam told me. We'll make him suffer for that man's death," I growled. He would have done the same to Toby, and I would make sure his last moments on the mortal plane were excruciating.

I heard Toby's footsteps coming up behind me, and Jude looked at me, but I only nodded for him to continue. I wouldn't hide anything from Toby. If he wanted to know what was going on, then he deserved that closure.

"I… Dex, I smelled another human on a lot of this guy's clothing. He lived alone, and according to all Liam's digging, he doesn't have a boyfriend or post about anyone on social media," Jude said.

"A coworker?" I asked.

"The other person smelled like fear and innocence, Dex," Jude answered.

Toby grabbed onto me from behind. "Do you think the other guy he stalked is still alive?" he gasped.

Jude shrugged. "I don't know. The scent wasn't fresh, but it wasn't so old that it had faded. There was no one in his ritzy apartment complex that fit the smell—I searched the halls on each floor to be sure. He's well off, and Liam is trying to find out if there are any other properties he owns. There's some family money, but most of the estate looks like it's lived in by other family members. If he has this guy stored somewhere, we have quite a few possibilities."

"So you'll find out," Toby answered. "You'll do whatever you need to in order to find out where this guy is, and you'll save him."

He kissed the back of my arm then, saying, "Go talk to him, Dex. I'm ok. Jude and Corbin are here with me."

I turned and pressed a kiss to his lips, then I jumped off his porch and stalked over to my house. Toby was right; I had work to do.

By the time I was in the door and walking down the basement

steps, the stench of the decaying soul was overpowering.

Atlas was in his human form, a pair of sweatpants and a hoodie that were obviously mine thrown on. He sat sulking in the corner, staring at the guy who was tied up and gagged in a chair. The guy was bruised and bleeding, and his wrist was definitely mangled, but he looked pretty intact otherwise.

"Thank you," I murmured to Atlas. He had saved Toby. He had taken care of things when I was too distracted, and he hadn't killed this guy when I would've because he had obviously been in touch with Jude.

Atlas merely grunted in acknowledgement. That was our Atlas—a hellhound of few words.

I took the gag out of the guy's mouth. "What's your name?" I asked, even though I could've just asked Jude.

"Bradley. Bradley Howard. I have money. My family has money. They'll pay a ransom for me," he rambled.

I laughed. "You think this is about money? You tried to kidnap Toby."

"I didn't," the man started, and I slapped him across the face. He whimpered even though it was barely a tap.

"My Toby," I snarled.

That seemed to shake something loose in him, because he stared at me hatefully.

"Did you think he was yours?" I snarled. "He isn't yours. He would never be yours. He would never stoop to a disgusting piece of shit like you. You aren't worth the ground he walks upon."

"I could've given him everything. He doesn't want you; he wants me! We're fated to be together!" the man yelled, spittle flying from his mouth.

"Just like the bartender? Is he fated to be with you, too?" I asked.

"Aiden and I broke up," Bradley said. "I would never cheat on Toby."

I'd seen all kinds of delusional shit, and I knew that this guy totally believed his break up story. The only question was whether or not Aiden was still alive, or if their "break up" meant that Bradley had killed him.

"Time for some answers, Bradley," I muttered, walking over to a table that had some tools laid out.

"Finally," Atlas muttered.

If Aiden was still alive, we'd find out where he was. If I happened to try out some more torture methods for my boyfriend along the way, well—anything for my Toby. I smiled as I turned around to face the piece of shit who had tried to hurt my Toby, and he whimpered at the look on my face.

"Don't worry, Bradley—I'm sure you'll tell us everything we need to know," I said, stalking toward him.

He was screaming within a minute, and Atlas and I found out everything we needed to within an hour. It didn't matter, though. He would've hurt Toby, and his suffering wasn't going to end that quickly.

We made it last.

Chapter 25

Corbin and Jude fed me and distracted me, and I talked to Amy, who was just fine, thank goodness. At some point I must have fallen asleep on the couch, because I woke up to Dex kneeling in front of me, gently caressing my hair. He was freshly showered, his hair still damp, and he was smiling softly at me.

"I love you," he murmured softly.

"I love you too, Dex," I answered. I sat up, blinking and rubbing my eyes. "Is it over?" I asked.

I didn't want details, but I needed to know.

Dex nodded his head.

"And the guy… " I trailed off, afraid of the answer.

"Jude and Corbin are headed to get him. We think he's still alive," Dex answered.

I shook my head, tears coming to my eyes. "That could've been me," I whispered.

Dex grabbed me and hugged me tightly, and I didn't know if it was for me or for him.

"What's his name?" I asked.

"Jude said his name is Aiden," Dex answered.

"We have to help him, Dex. Promise me we'll help him," I said. "I have money…"

"Money isn't an issue. Jude and Corbin will bring him back here and we'll see from there. He might have family he wants to go back to. We'll make sure he gets whatever he needs. Don't worry," Dex assured me.

"When will you know?" I asked. I meant when would he know if the guy was alive, and Dex seemed to realize that.

"Jude will call as soon as they get there," he answered.

He sat next to me on the couch, and we just sort of cuddled for a while. It felt really nice, but I knew we were both waiting for his phone to ring. When it finally did, I almost jumped out of my skin.

"Yeah," he answered.

I couldn't hear the other side of the conversation, but his hand squeezed mine, and he nodded as he listened while Jude apparently filled him in.

"Good. I'm glad. What now?" Dex asked.

There was a pause as Dex listened, and this time I squeezed his hand. I felt like we were responsible for this guy, even though I knew that wasn't rational. "Tell them to bring him here," I whispered.

He listened again and then said, "Yeah. We'll find him a good home. I have experience in placing strays."

He rolled his eyes at whatever Jude said, then he hung up the phone.

"So, the guy is ok. He's probably malnourished and dehydrated, but he doesn't appear to be wounded other than that. They asked him about family or anyone looking for him, and it didn't seem like that was the case. They debated bringing him to the human police, but Jude heard your suggestion and agreed. He said the guy isn't very responsive and is probably in shock. My guess is that it hasn't sunk in that he's actually safe. The human police would probably just further traumatize him," Dex explained.

I thought about that. The police were the best option. But this guy hadn't had a say in anything that had happened to him for a year. When he got here, we'd let him decide.

"How long until they get back?" I asked.

"Couple hours. They're going to have him shower and eat before coming back." Dex looked at me then, and I saw a spark in his eyes. "Atlas is gone, too. It's just us."

If he had asked me a half hour ago, I would've said there wasn't a sexy thought in my head. But now, knowing that it was really over, that the stalker was gone, that the guy he'd kidnapped was safe—I felt this profound sense of relief, and more than anything, I wanted to be close to Dex.

He growled low in his throat—and I felt myself getting hard at the sound.

"My Toby," he grumbled, and I nodded my head yes.

He picked me up off the couch, and fuck, he was fast. He ran up the stairs and into my bedroom, slamming the door shut with a flick of his hips. He slowed down then, kissing me as I wrapped my legs around his waist. Our lips pressed together, and all the stress of the last day melted away with each flick of tongue, each nibble of lips.

We started slowly, tenderly, but before long we were both frantic, gasping for breath as our lips slanted against each other. I rubbed up against Dex as much as I could while being held up by him, but I needed skin to skin.

"Need you, Dex," I cried out. "Need to feel your skin. Need to feel you inside me."

Dex turned and laid me gently on the bed, then he hurriedly stripped out of his clothes. I fumbled with my own clothes, somehow getting my shirt stuck over my head. Dex chuckled and pulled off my pants, and I attempted my own growly sound at him.

I'm not sure it worked, since he just chuckled again, but he helped disentangle me, and then he stretched out on top of me, his face pressed close to mine.

"You're so fucking cute, Toby. And you're mine, and I love you, and I will kill anyone who tries to hurt you," he murmured.

"You say the sweetest stuff, Dex," I murmured, smiling and running my hands through his hair. "I love you, too. And you're mine, just as much as I'm yours."

"Yes," he growled as he kissed me again, running his hands along my back and then to my chest, tweaking my nipples and caressing my skin.

And that's when I felt… something bumping against my hole.

Only…

"Dex?" I asked, pulling my mouth away from his. "Do you have extra hands or something, because they're up here, so what's down there?"

He grinned down at me, and… whatever it was gently flicked against my hole. Fuck. It felt like a finger, only thicker, and it seemed lubed up already. It gently caressed me, and it felt so good, but his hands were still both here, and his dick was hard against my thigh, so it wasn't that.

I was turned on and confused by equal measures. If there was a ghost or something prodding at my hole, I thought that might be enough to pull me from the sexy moment.

Maybe. I mean, it was Dex, so maybe not.

"Hellhounds have tails," Dex murmured, and he took that moment to let the tip of his tail slip inside me.

"Oh god," I murmured, because it felt so fucking good.

"Is that ok?" he whispered.

I looked up to see hesitation in his face, but at the same time his tail thrust deeper, found my prostate, and pressed. My eyes slid shut in bliss.

"Oh god, yes, yes, definitely ok. Better than ok. So good. Dex!" I cried out as I felt sparks of pleasure flow through my whole body as his tail undulated inside me, rubbing against my channel, nudging into my prostate.

I opened my eyes to see him grinning down at me. "I also have a knot," he murmured. "Usually I can control it and not knot someone…"

"Oh my god, last time—you knotted me?" I asked, remembering how he had felt bigger, how we had been so blissed out in pleasure for so long.

"I can try to hold it back…" he started, but I interrupted him.

"You better fucking knot me, Dex. I want it all," I insisted, then I cried out again as his tail did whatever the fuck it was doing inside me, making me feel like a bundle of sexual nerves.

His lips were on mine again, and I was grabbing onto him, scratching him, but it only seemed to turn him on more as his tail pushed deeper and his hands touched every inch of me. He ground into me, his cock hard against my thigh and his stomach muscles rippling with each thrust, applying pressure against my own dick.

I was going to come, my god, I was going to come from his tail inside me and his scent around me and his hands on me.

"Dex!" I cried out, and my dick spasmed as I came onto his stomach.

"Yes, baby. So beautiful. So pretty in your pleasure," Dex murmured, continuing to rub against me, drawing out the pleasure.

Eventually he stopped his movements, but he was still hard against me, and his tail was still in me. He kissed me everywhere—my face, my neck, my chest—his hands gently soothing me. He skimmed his lips back up my neck and along my jaw, meeting my lips with another sweet kiss, our tongues lightly dancing against each other.

We kissed for an eternity, and I reveled in his skin against mine, the feeling of being surrounded by him. I shifted my hips and felt his tail in me, and a spark of pleasure floated down my spine.

"Dex," I whispered. God, I didn't think I could be ready again so quickly, but I wanted him in me. I needed it. I needed to feel him.

"I'm here, baby," he said.

"Need you inside me," I murmured, caressing his face. He was so beautiful and sexy, and he was mine. God, I loved this man. I loved this hellhound.

He slowly withdrew his tail from me—and I was definitely gonna see that later, because holy fuck they had held out on me when they neglected to mention the whole tail thing amidst all my questions. I hadn't thought to ask, but still… that was an important detail!

He slid his body up, his arms holding him up over me, and dear god he was so unbelievably sexy. How had I gotten so fucking lucky? He was hot as hell and protective in the best way and he talked to me about all my weird writer stuff and he loved me. He was perfect for me.

"I love you so much, Dex," I said.

He slid into me in one agonizingly slow thrust, and I couldn't help closing my eyes and mewling. There was a slight burning, but it was all pleasure and the exquisite feeling of being full of Dex, of being joined together.

When I opened my eyes he was staring down at me, flames licking in his eyes.

"Mine," he rumbled, and was it weird that I found it crazy hot that he was so turned on he sounded like he was barely holding onto his human form?

"Yes," I said simply.

"Love you," he rumbled, and then he started moving.

Oh. My. God.

He stared into my eyes as he gently rolled his hips, and I couldn't look away from the flames burning there. He looked at me like I was the entire world, and it melted my heart. I lifted my hand to caress his cheek.

"Yours," I said simply. "Always yours. Forever, Dex."

He growled, and we stared at one another until the intensity was almost too much to bear.

The pleasure gently rolled through me, growing deeper and deeper. Pleasure licked along my skin, and I saw blue flames surrounding both of us, but it didn't hurt. It was like feathers gently caressing me, and it only heightened the sensations.

He thickened inside me, and holy fuck—that was his knot. I was going to make him come. He was going to knot me. It was sexy as fuck.

"Dex!' I cried out, my orgasm surprising me as it crashed into me.

He grew thicker and thicker—fuck, so full. I didn't know if I could take it, and yet somehow I did, and I felt like my orgasm just kept going on and on and on.

His hips barely moved, just a gentle push and pull as he filled me up, and his teeth grazed against my neck, but I wanted his bite. I wanted his teeth in me.

"Yes," I cried out, incapable of saying more, but he knew.

He bit down, thrust his hips into me, and I swear I could feel his seed filling me up. As he spilled into me, my blood trickled into him, and I thought of our bodies connecting in an unbreakable loop.

We were one, tied together in pleasure and love. The pleasure went on and on until I thought I'd die from it, and at some point I felt like I separated from my body, floating in a haze. It was too much, too perfect, too beautiful.

Dex was mine. Forever. That was my last thought as I drifted away on a cloud of ecstasy.

CHAPTER 26

DEXTER

I don't know how long my knot lasted, but the pleasure was beyond anything I had ever known. I gently lapped at Toby's neck as my knot went down, and he murmured happily. He smelled like bliss and contentment and pleasure, and I tucked my head into his neck, inhaling deeply.

He smelled like he was mine.

We laid together, holding one another, and eventually when my knot went down I gently pulled out of him. He made a small sound of protest, but he was already half asleep, and we both drifted off, wrapped around each other.

The sound of car doors woke me briefly some time later, and when Jude spoke from outside, I could hear him clear enough.

"Aiden is sleeping. I'll let you know when he wakes," Jude said. I heard one of them walk inside with a heavier footfall—probably carrying the man—and the other follow behind.

It was still dark out, and Toby was resting peacefully beside me. I brushed my hand through his hair. He was mortal, just like that man who had been carried inside. He was mortal, and I was not. I didn't think I'd really grasped what that meant until his stalker had found him.

Some day Toby would die.

Hopefully I would have decades with him, but some day I wouldn't have him anymore. That was the nature of mortality.

I didn't think I could bear it. I loved Toby more than I'd ever loved anything in my entire existence. He was more to me than my pack, more than anything in my life. I would give everything up for Toby.

If he died someday, then I would find a way to follow him into the afterlife. I could not contemplate the thought of being separated from him. I would find a way for us to always be together.

With that thought, and a press of my lips against his skin, I let myself fall back to sleep.

Toby's breathing changed, and I woke instantly. I was on immediate alert, but he was only waking up. I gently caressed his skin, and he rolled into me, smiling against my chest.

"Good morning, baby," I murmured.

He pressed a kiss against my skin, and I growled, unable to help myself.

"Are you purring?" Toby asked, giggling.

"I… Am I what?" I asked. "I'm not… I'm not a cat. I'm a hellhound. We don't purr."

Toby chuckled into my chest, clearly delighted at my response.

"I am… I am growling," I added.

"Nah. Growling is scary. This is all soft and happy," Toby argued.

I thought for a moment. Ok, perhaps he had a point. Still, hellhounds did not purr.

"I am rumbling in pleasure," I finally settled on.

Toby laughed again. "Well, I love your rumbles, my sexy neighbor."

"Your sexy boyfriend," I corrected.

"How about just mine," Toby said, looking up at me and pulling my head down for a quick peck.

"Yes," I rumbled in approval. I liked being Toby's. Before I could pull him in for another kiss, Toby jumped out of bed.

"Hey," I protested, but he just started rifling through his drawers and pulling on clothes.

"Later," he answered. "Your brothers must be back by now."

"They are," I admitted. "They got home in the night. The guy was sleeping."

"Well, we're going to go over and check on him," Toby insisted.

I supposed that was the proper thing to do.

We managed to get dressed with only a minimal amount of kissing and caressing, and we walked over to my house hand-in-hand. When we walked up the steps and into the house, I could hear Jude and Corbin in the kitchen, and even Toby inhaled deeply at the smell of breakfast cooking.

The man was sitting on the couch under a blanket, even though it wasn't cold. He was thin, and his head was shaved clean. He had eyes that seemed too big for his face, and I could tell that he was very attractive, despite the obvious trauma he'd been through. He didn't even look over at us.

Toby walked over slowly and sat in a chair across from the guy.

"Hi Aiden. I'm Toby," he said.

The man jerked at that, finally looking over at Toby.

"You're safe?" the man asked.

"Yes. He didn't get me. He tried, but he didn't get me," Toby said.

"Good," Aiden said, looking at me. "He talked a lot about you at the end. He said he wouldn't kick me out, and until you decided to move in with him, I could stay."

Toby looked like he didn't know what to say to that.

The man turned and looked off into the distance. "I knew he would probably kill me. I knew that from the moment he told me he was 'breaking up' with me. I didn't want him to get someone else, but at the same time, I hoped… I hoped maybe it would give me a chance to get away." He looked back at Toby then. "I'm sorry."

Toby reached forward tentatively with his hand extended in invitation. The man flinched a little, but then he reached out and let Toby hold his hand.

"None of this is your fault," Toby insisted. "None of it. And it's ok that you hoped for that. Anything that went through your head is ok. Do you understand?"

Aiden stared at him, but eventually he nodded his head.

"He's dead," I said.

They both looked over at me, and Aiden tilted his head. I could smell his disbelief.

"I killed him. He suffered," I added.

Toby flinched a bit and looked over at Aiden, worried. Oops. Was I not supposed to tell the man that?

Aiden eventually nodded his head, though. "Good," he said, then he let Toby's hand go and gripped his blanket again.

"You have choices," Toby said. "We can get the police involved, but he is dead, and they'll never find him, and we'll deny the fact that we killed him."

Awww, look at Toby being all protective of us, like we couldn't handle the human police. Still, it was super cute.

"Or," Toby continued, "we can bring you home, back to your life."

Aiden snorted at that. "What life? I was a bartender. No family. No boyfriend. He knew all that. Friends, sure, but they gave up soon enough. Sure, people looked for me, but after a year… there's no one left looking for me. He let me look it up. He let me search articles and the internet. He was trying to show me that no one but him cared about me. And really, I'm not the man I was before. I wouldn't even know who to be with my friends. They wouldn't know me now. I don't know myself."

Toby looked stumped at that, but I jumped in.

"That's ok. We can give you a place to stay, a job, and new people. You can take your time finding out who you are now," I said.

He looked over at me. "You want me to stay here?"

"You could stay in this house, but I think I have an even better solution," I said. When the man nodded, I went out to the porch.

Time to call the oracle. Surely the first stray and this one could bond over their human trauma and stuff.

Cassius strangely hadn't sounded excited to hear from me. When I told him I had another human who had been held prisoner, he had told me to bring the guy over, muttering something about not trusting me with humans.

I resented that. I always found them good homes.

Toby had insisted on coming along, and his presence seemed to set Aiden at ease, so the three of us headed out in the car. Although Jude and Corbin had rescued him, Aiden hadn't seemed attached to them in the least. I wasn't sure if that was because they'd shown some of their hellhound abilities or not, but he also didn't seem scared of them. He just seemed indifferent.

So it was just the three of us that walked into Cass's shop that afternoon. The guy from the basement was at the counter when we walked in, and he gave us all a glower. Good to see he was still feeling feisty. Maybe he'd spread some of that energy to this guy.

Cassius hurried out, saying, "Q, be nice. Aiden is going to stay with us for a bit. He's got a similar story to yours."

"What, he was held captive in a basement?" Q snarked.

Aiden looked at him oddly, then said, "No, it was a bedroom with bars on the window."

That seemed to shut Q right up, and he eventually nodded at Aiden.

Cassius's angel mate stepped out of the back then, and he walked over to Aiden. He murmured something, and he led Aiden into the back. He went, stopping at the door.

"Thank you," he said to us simply. Then he looked at Toby. "I'm glad he didn't get you, and I'm glad he's dead."

Toby just nodded.

Once they were in the back, Q said, "Fuck, man, you find all the trouble."

I shrugged, saying, "I find humans in need of good homes."

"Jesus, we aren't cats," Q muttered, and then he went into the back as well.

I just blinked, looking at Toby. "I know they aren't cats. Why does everyone keep comparing stray humans to cats? I think it's disrespectful."

Toby just laughed and kissed me lightly, and Cassius sighed happily from the counter.

"Oh, I do love a happy ending. I knew it would all work out. You two are so good together," he murmured.

A happy ending… for now. Because Toby would die someday, but maybe Cassius could help with that.

"So…" I started, glancing at Toby, unsure how to continue. I didn't want to bring up his mortality and make him worry.

"What? What's worrying you?" Toby asked.

"You're mortal," I answered. "I could have lost you to the stalker. You could get hurt, or get sick, and I don't think…" I trailed off, unable to continue.

Toby's face fell, and he reached out to grab my hand.

Cassius, however, just snorted.

"Oh, you two, don't go getting all maudlin on me," Cassius answered, starting to wipe down the counter. "As if you could be separated," he muttered under his breath.

We both looked over at him, surprised.

"Uh, we can't?" Toby asked.

Cassius snorted. "Of course you can't. He marked you." Cassius gestured vaguely between us, but I really had no idea what he was talking about.

He obviously figured that out, because he rolled his eyes. Toby was looking at me all hopefully, and I was staring at Cassius, waiting for him to explain.

"I have no idea what you're talking about," I answered.

"You think someone would have filled you in. You marked and mated him, Dexter. That means your life forces are tied together. Where one goes, the other goes. He couldn't have died out in the woods, because I'm pretty sure you marked him before that. The beginnings of the bond were already forming last time I saw him," Cassius explained.

Toby and I stared at each other for a moment of frozen time, and then we crashed together in a rush, relief flowing through us both.

"Supernatural beings and afterlifers. You'd really think you'd know a little more about your own capabilities," he muttered. "Leave it to the oracle to always clean up after everyone else's mess."

When I finally pulled away from Toby, I looked over to see him grinning at us despite his snark.

"Thank you, Cassius," I said.

He nodded at us both. "I'll take care of Aiden. Off with you two. I'm sure you have some more marking to do." He winked and went back to cleaning up, and although I was tempted to throw Toby over my shoulder in order to get him back to my house, somehow we managed a rather fast walk back to the car instead.

Mine. Toby was really mine forever. And I was his.

Apparently I loved happy endings too, because I couldn't stop grinning the entire way home.

EPILOGUE

I finished writing my final scene in my book. I also loved a happy ending—I guess that was why I was a writer. I sighed as I shut my laptop, and Dex came over to snuggle me on the couch. He was great about letting me work, but he was also great about knowing when I needed a break.

It hadn't even seemed like a question for him to start staying with me. I know we probably should have had a discussion about it or something, but whatever. I kept putting his stuff in drawers and in my closet when he grabbed clothes for the next morning. He didn't mention that, although he smiled every time he saw something folded or hanging up. I didn't mention that he brought over more than he needed for the next day each night. I figured at some point we'd talk about it, but not even a week had passed since the whole stalker thing, so we had time.

Apparently we had all the time in the world, which was kind of cool.

Dex had a moment where he thought maybe I would be freaked out by the whole marking thing, but I laid that to rest with a hardcore make-out session and a demand for his tail and knot, because that would never get old. It was hot as fuck, and I definitely had a new series in my future.

Dex was great for providing inspiration. Especially for sex scenes.

Jude and Corbin had pretty much moved into his house, and I knew they went hunting, or whatever they wanted to call it, in the nearby cities. Dex had been hesitant to leave me, but I had kissed him and told him to go to work and that I would be fine, and I had stayed up most of the night writing. I knew he'd made Jude and Corbin stay next door to keep an ear on me, and I didn't mind.

When he'd come home with his shirt missing—probably burned off to get rid of the blood, I guessed—I hadn't been able to help jumping him in the shower. He was making the world a better place, and if he had to torture and maim people to do it… Well, I was a pretty gory writer, and I didn't mind. They were, after all, very bad people.

"I'm done," I finally admitted. It was always sort of bittersweet to finish a novel.

"Amazing! I'm so proud of you!" Dex said, kissing my forehead. "Let's celebrate!"

I sighed. "Yeah. I mean there's still editing and having my beta readers go through it, and who knows how much I'll have to change…"

Dex took my face in his hands and looked into my eyes. "Toby, you're amazing. I'm sure your book is amazing, and you finished. That's awesome."

I smiled. I guessed it kind of was.

"Let's go see Jude and Corbin. They're usually cooking up something good for lunch," I added.

Dex nodded, then added, "Liam got here, too."

I gasped, and Dex looked alarmed.

"What?! Liam is here?" I cried out. "Your other brother… err, packmate… got here, and you didn't tell me? Dex! You have to introduce me!" I insisted.

I loved Dex, I really did, but he was a little clueless sometimes. I got up and started up the stairs. I had to shower and find something to wear. I was going to meet more of Dex's family, and I wanted to make a good impression.

Dex just sat on the couch looking confused. I almost chuckled at him, then I thought about dragging him upstairs with me, and he must have smelled that idea, because I heard a low growl, but I stopped him before he even got up.

"Nope. Nuh uh. Not happening right now, my sexy mate. I have to get ready, and I am not having my first introduction to Liam be after he heard us having sex," I insisted. "Hellhound hearing," I muttered, before making my way into the bathroom for a quick shower. Sometimes it was kind of annoying knowing that they could all hear and smell every-thing, but I guess that was my life now.

I definitely wasn't complaining.

By the time I made my way downstairs, it was after lunch, but Dex assured me that his brothers had just started cooking. I decided not to ask if that was because they'd heard us or because he had called. Some things were better left unknown.

We walked over hand-in-hand to Dex's house. Well, his old house, because he was definitely moving in with me.

We didn't knock, because it was Dex's house. Plus, I'm sure they heard us coming anyways. Liam was, of course, sexy as hell, because apparently that was a prerequisite for hellhounds. He was sitting at the kitchen table at a computer, although he closed it when we walked in. He looked more sophisticated than Jude and Corbin, wearing a white button down and playing with electronics, but I could see that hell-hound gleam in his eyes. He couldn't fool me.

"Hi! I'm Toby!" I said, although I didn't walk forward to shake or anything, mainly because Dex was holding onto me.

"Yes, I know," Liam responded. "I enjoyed your books. I've also changed the address on your newsletter and made your website more secure."

Okey-dokey then. I just nodded my head. I had a feeling having a hacker hellhound would prove to be useful.

Jude and Corbin brought food over to the table, and Dex and I grabbed plates and silverware. It wasn't long before we were all sitting and sharing a meal, making small talk.

"How are the stray humans settling in?" Dex eventually asked. Jude had said he was going to visit the coffee shop yesterday, so that was probably why Dex brought it up. Everyone seemed to roll their eyes at Dex's word choice, but I just smiled.

"They seem ok, I guess. They both seem wary of me," Jude said, looking a little offended. He did look like the boy next door, but we all knew he was a lot more than that.

"Quinton and Aiden will be fine," Liam said, and everyone stopped to stare at him.

He seemed to notice, because he looked up and raised an eyebrow.

"Q's name is Quinton?" I asked. I don't think any of us had known that, and a look around the table confirmed that, because everyone looked like it was news to them.

"Yes. Don't worry about them. I'm keeping a close eye on things. Aiden is in therapy, but Quinton refuses to go. He has some troubling browser searches, but I'll take care of it," Liam said, taking a bite of sausage and chewing.

The other hellhounds just nodded and went back to eating, but I stared at him. "Are you… watching them?" I asked.

"Of course," he replied, continuing to eat. "But don't worry—I made sure no one else can keep an eye on them. Especially since it seems like Quinton's abductor wasn't alone in his sex trafficking."

Everyone paused at that, and I could hear some low growling from around the table.

"I'll protect him," Liam insisted, and I heard a growl behind his words as flames lit up in his eyes. "I'm already looking into it. We'll find everyone involved, and we'll make them pay for what they did to him."

That seemed to settle everyone down, and we went back to eating.

I kept stealing glances at Liam, though. He may have looked all polished and sophisticated, but I knew exactly what hellhounds were capable of. I hoped he didn't scare Q too much if he decided to ask the man some questions. They could all be a little… intense.

We finished our meal and moved on to lighter topics. Liam asked about Atlas, but we hadn't seen him since last week. No one seemed concerned, so I didn't worry either.

The brothers, or packmates, continued to eat long after I was done, and I just sat and smiled at the moment. Jude hummed a Beatles song, Corbin fed a crow under the table, and Liam had opened his laptop back up to glance at it occasionally as he ate. They talked about cities nearby and the best routes to get there for hunting, and although it was totally strange, it was also totally comforting.

This was my life now. It was like I had ended up in one of my own books. I looked over at Dex, who was already staring at me with love in his eyes. A spark of flame lit up inside them, and I couldn't help the pulse of arousal that went through me. Dex did that sexy not purring thing (although it totally sounded like purring), and his brothers ignored us both.

Before I could even protest, he stood up, picked me up in his arms, and stalked toward the door, leaning in to kiss me as he walked.

I heard Jude catcall behind us, and Corbin and Liam laughed, but I ignored them all. "Don't forget to turn on the music," I murmured as we walked across the yard back to my house, and Dex's eyes danced with flames.

I couldn't believe how lucky I was. I guess sometimes fantasies did come true, even if they were in the form of hellhound serial killers who flirted by talking about torture. I snorted a little with that thought, but Dex continued to not purr as he carried me up the stairs and into the bedroom.

"I love you, my mate," he whispered in my ear, giving the mark on my neck a little nibble.

"I love you, Dex. Forever," I murmured back. "And I better get your knot," I added.

Dex chuckled as we fell onto the bed together, and I delighted in making him laugh. We may have had forever to be together, but I would still cherish every moment and every laugh with my hellhound.

HOW TO HACK A HELLHOUND

QUINTON

Getting kidnapped and held hostage in a human trafficker's basement was not on my bingo card. Getting rescued by a paranormal being was also not on my bingo card. (Apparently I needed to trade in bingo cards.) The guy who took me may be dead, but I know there are more people behind the operation, and I plan to shut it down. If I need to get the help of one of the creepy glowing eyed dudes to do it, I will. It turns out Liam is incredibly sexy and really good with technology, too. He may be great at hacking into computers, but I'm determined to hack my way into his life.

LIAM

Ever since I looked into the feisty human that Dexter rescued from a basement, I've been a little… obsessed. Is it wrong that I watch him all the time and hack into all his technology? I'm just trying to keep him safe. After all, he's sticking his nose into some troubling areas, and I can't deal with the thought of him getting taken again. Of course I offer to help him when I discover his mission to take down a trafficking ring, although my motives aren't exactly pure. The little human attracts me in a way that I can't explain, and my hellhound thinks he's mine, whether he wants to be or not.

Tags: Emotionally traumatized, feisty vigilante and hacker hellhound fall in love; Liam has Quinton under surveillance 24/7 and will protect him; Quinton doesn't mind being watched if the dude with the glowing eyes will keep him safe; there's torture and death (but only of really bad people); hellhounds have tails, and they know how to use them.

Author's Note

Dear Reader,

Once again, thank you for coming on this wild ride with me. Dexter and Toby were so much fun to write, and for those of you who saw the meme about a writer and a serial killer, yes, I definitely took inspiration from that. I wanted to write something a little darker, but as you can tell, I can't quite be too dark—I'm a little too squeamish for that. So although there's lots of discussion about torture and such, those scenes always end up not occurring on page.

If you're curious about Cassius and Kushiel, they are from the Demonic Disasters and Afterlife Adventures series, and their story is in A Beginner's Guide to Ghosts, Fallen Angels, and Other Afterlifers. Cassius sees ghosts and is an oracle, and Kushiel is an angel who feels like he has no place. Cassius is always helpful, and he pops up in quite a few other books as well.

For future books in the series, I have some more traumatized characters coming up. No one's trauma is ever exactly the same, and I'll do my best to give the characters the forum they need to express their hurt, but please know that no human ever reacts the same to what happens to them. Also know that those books will be more about their healing journey than a focus on what was done to them. It shaped who they are, but we are all more than what has happened to us.

If you hadn't guessed, Q is up next. You'll find out more about his background and how exactly he ended up in that cellar. Josh, Sebbie, and Aiden will also eventually find their own happy endings, so don't worry about them. They might have to fight to get there, but they'll all come out stronger on the other side. Happy endings are always guaranteed with me.

If you enjoyed this book, please leave a review. Reviews are the lifeblood of self-published authors. Every time I see my books recommended, get an email from a fan, or read a positive review, it lights me up and keeps me writing. This wouldn't be possible without all of you cheering me on.

Happy Reading!
Shannon Mae

About the Author

Shannon Mae began her journey in the M/M romance world as an avid reader, then a beta reader, and eventually an editor who works with the unparalleled Tammy B. PA from Aspen Tree E.A.S.

When a dear friend suggested she should write her own book, she decided to do just that. She gravitates to writing paranormal romance, since that genre is her first love, and her books tend to be low-angst and filled with happily-ever-afters.

She is an unfailing optimist with a side of snark and sarcasm. When she isn't editing, writing, or working her day job, which she loves, you'll find her on some outdoor adventure or embarking on a hands-on project (that is probably slightly more complex than she thought it was).

She lives in a small, seaside town on the east coast, and she spends her free time with her eye-rolling, sassy teenage daughter and her adorably loving dog.

Life is a place full of mysteries and wonders, and she hopes to capture that joy and fun in her writing. Adding some fun, sexy times makes it all complete.

Shannon Mae loves hearing from readers!

ALSO BY SHANNON MAE

DEMONIC DISASTERS AND AFTERLIFE ADVENTURES: (PARANORMAL ROMANCE)

A Beginner's Guide to Death, Demons, and Other Afterlife Disasters
A Beginner's Guide to Mistakenly Summoned Demons and Other Misadventures
A Beginner's Guide to the Care and Feeding of Pet Demons (A Novella)
A Beginner's Guide to Revenge, Chaos, and Other Absurd Escapades
A Beginner's Guide to Demonic Possessions (A Novella)
A Beginner's Guide to Christmas Miracles (A Holiday Novella)

Collections:
Demonic Disasters and Afterlife Adventures Collection 1

HELLHOUNDS OF PARADISE FALLS: (PARANORMAL ROMANCE)

How to Flirt with a Hellhound
How to Hack a Hellhound